HIGH IRON TO FAIRBANKS
Building the Historic Alaska Railroad

ISBN: 978-1-57833-643-2

Library of Congress Control Number: 2016909948

Book design: Vered Mares, Todd Communications
Cover Design: Debra Dubac, Todd Communications

Printed by United Graphics, LLC
through Alaska Print Brokers, Anchorage, Alaska.

Published by

MISSION MOUNTAIN BOOKS
PO Box 1101
Polson, MT 59860
Visit www.highirontofairbanks.com
for additional information on this publication.

Distributed by:
Todd Communications
611 E. 12th Ave.
Anchorage, Alaska 99501-4603
Phone: **(907) 274-TODD (8633)** • Fax: (907) 929-5550
WWW.ALASKABOOKSANDCALENDARS.COM • sales@toddcom.com
with other offices in Juneau and Fairbanks, Alaska

Table of Contents

HIGH IRON TO FAIRBANKS

Preface

My fascination with the Alaska Railroad began with a train ride to visit friends at a remote cabin north of Talkeetna in November of 1974, and evolved in to a relationship over the next three decades. I did audit work at the federally-owned Alaska Railroad in the 1970s, served on the team coordinating the transfer of ownership to the State of Alaska in the 1980s and worked for the state-owned Railroad in the 1990s. Because I couldn't be trusted with machinery I was, unfortunately, stuck with a desk job

My knowledge of the railroad's early history was limited, until retirement gave me the time to study that fascinating historic period. My reading led to a volume of notes that became a story of the construction years. When family suggested that the story was very boring I added offbeat characters and told the story in a fictional format, but attempted to portray historical events and people with reasonable accuracy. Clearly, dialog attributed to historical figures is the product of my imagination. Poetic Pete's verse is entirely the inspiration of the Robert W. Service works that I learned to love during my years in the land of the midnight sun.

I take full credit for grammatical, spelling and other errors that escaped the competent eyes of great editors. My story is that I've deliberately left a few blunders as a tribute to all of the teachers who tried in vain to learn me how to right write.

HIGH IRON TO FAIRBANKS

PART ONE
Establishing the Route
(1914)

SS Dirigo

H.C. Barley Photographs,
UAF-1981-193-2, Archives, University of Alaska Fairbanks

Chapter One

The job went well until the firing. "You have a good head and you work hard," the foreman said. It was Mac's only thank you for his years of service to the Tanana Valley Railroad. "Stay sober and you'll find other work soon enough."

The exhausting job had kept Mac's bottle habit at bay, but his demons preyed on idle time. When news of government plans to build a railroad in Alaska reached Fairbanks he'd acquired a string of pack horses and traveled down to Ship Creek Landing to await the railroad builders.

Today, June 6, 1914, he sat alone on the bluff above the creek watching its clear waters end their mountain to sea journey, devoured by the silt-laden estuary. The insipid mud bordering the tidal zone muted the bright green leaves and white bark of the trees growing astride the alluvial bottomland. Beyond, the gray Cook Inlet waters ebbed and flowed; silent unseen forces pushing one way and then the other. *Lifelike,* he thought.

When he spotted the *SS Dirigo* on the horizon Mac knew his wait was over. The sun peaked, then drifted back northward as the steam-driven vessel moved slowly landward, struggling against the strong tidal currents. The well-seasoned Alaskan watched the boat approach and eagerly awaited the next chapter of his life. *Could this new government railroad project quell the ebbs and flows that had become the hallmark of his existence?*

I'll be go to hell, a floating rodeo, Mac thought, watching five all-too-tidy men struggle with the skittish horses they were lightering ashore on a small barge. "Lend a hand?" he asked, as the seagoing corral slid aground on the muddy shore.

"Sure can," said one of the men, "if you know anything about horses."

Mac nodded a silent yes, and with confident authority stroked the bay mare's neck and quietly took control of the big animal, demonstrating that his penchant for western garb wasn't just for show. "Where you taking them?"

"Away from the water and away from this damn mud," the man said. "I'm Charles Jones with the United States Government."

"My name's Frank McDonald, but most folks call me Mac." His father's name was Frank as well and as a boy he'd been called Junior, but when he grew a head taller than his dad he'd become 'Mac.' He still thought of his father as the bigger man, though he'd received word of his death several years prior.

Jones looked up. "Pleased to meet you. What's a cowboy doing up here in Alaska?"

Mac knew the tall hat accentuated his loftiness, and spoke to his background. "I've liked working with horses since I was a kid, and being up here in Alaska doesn't change that, just means that for part of the year I trade this big hat for one with ear flaps, and wear long-handled underwear."

"Well, we sure as hell could use some cowboy help. We've got twenty horses all together. First thing we have to do is stake them out until we can get a pen built."

Mac pointed toward his camp. "I just set up a temporary corral over by the bluff. I can put these wobbly-legged critters of yours in with my horses for the time being if you like."

"Thank you kindly," said Jones. "They've been on the boat for days. As soon as they get their legs back they'll be fine. And, the government will certainly pay you fairly for the use of your corral."

"No payment necessary," Mac said as they began moving the animals toward the small enclosure. With the horses safely penned, fed and watered, Mac pitched in unloading lumber and supplies, and this time he didn't object when Jones assured him the government would pay him for his time.

The sun was still well above the northern horizon as Mac rekindled the camp fire near his tent late that evening, the cargo finally ashore. He loved the summer sun, and the energy it gave. Tonight's low sun angle cast a golden hue across the turbid Cook Inlet waters, creating a warm glow that mirrored his mood.

The inlet is fifteen miles wide off the mouth of Ship Creek, before separating into two ever-narrowing branches. Turnagain Arm extends some forty odd miles through the mountains to the south and east toward Seward. Knik Arm reaches a similar distance to the north and east toward the Matanuska coal fields. A few miles to the east the towering Chugach Mountains form the third side of a large triangle of bench land, covered with birch, aspen and black spruce, dotted with small lakes and laced together by a network of pristine streams.

The government men struck Mac as a serious lot, in Alaska with a job to do. They pitched their tents near his camp, between the corral and the stream, and he invited them to join him for an end-of-day meal. He cooked a large salmon and after a week of ship-board victuals, followed by a day of hard labor, his new friends ate ravenously. "Good of you to share your meal with us," said Jones.

"The Athabaskans say if you hide what you catch you are not worthy to live among other people," said Mac.

"Good advice," said Jones. "Sounds like you've been in Alaska a long time."

"Arrived at the Klondike, over in the Yukon, back in '99," said Mac, "too late to get rich but soon enough to get gold fever. Chased the gold out to Nome and then to Fairbanks but drank and gambled away anything I found. I eventually took a job with the Tanana Valley Railroad. The hard work kept me sober and the steady pay kept me well fed, but they're going broke now and laying off all their help. Which makes me have to ask, why in damnation has the government decided to build a railroad in Alaska?"

"Good question," said Jones. "A couple years back a presidential commission reported that rail connections with year-round Alaskan ports are needed to develop the Territory's resources. President

Taft agreed, sort of. He believed the government should build the railroad but he opposed government operation. But, it didn't really matter what he wanted since he wasn't re-elected and the Congressional act passed this spring authorized the new President to locate and construct a railroad in the Territory of Alaska. It also authorized the government to operate the railroad."

Mac took off his hat and scratched his head. "Seems a bit peculiar that Congress has decided to build and operate the railroad, before they even know where the line will run from, and to."

Jones paused for a moment. "Well, they did provide some direction. The railroad can't be more than a thousand miles long and must connect at least one open Pacific harbor with the coal fields, and with navigable rivers. The total cost can't exceed thirty-five million dollars, and they already appropriated one million to get the project started."

"They must be serious," said Mac, "if they've already put up the money."

"They are very serious. In fact, this new President, Woodrow Wilson, already authorized the Interior Secretary to go ahead with the location surveys, and set up the Alaska Engineering Commission."

"I didn't know Alaska had an engineering commission."

"They don't. The commission is a federal organization, appointed by Washington. But, one of the commissioners, Tom Riggs, surveyed the Alaskan-Canadian boundary from the sea to the Arctic Ocean."

Like many Alaskans, Mac was growing suspicious of guidance from those with little knowledge of the territory. "So one member of the Alaska Engineering Commission has actually been to Alaska. What about the others?"

"There are two others. Lieutenant Frederick Mears was an engineer on the Great Northern Railway and helped build the Panama Railroad. William Edes located and built rail lines in the American West for many years."

Mac, less than a day full of this new job under his belt, was already concerned about where this journey might lead. "So has this new commission actually done anything?"

"Oh yes," Jones said. "Just a month ago they were authorized to select assistants and purchase materials and get on up here. They set up offices in Seattle and had us on our way to Ship Creek in short order. But we're just an advance party, we've got more horses and supplies on the way, and some mules too. We'll have well over one hundred head here before long and we'll buy more if we can."

"When do we start building this railroad?" asked Mac.

"First, we have to select the best of two possible routes, both running from tidewater up to Fairbanks. The eastern route starts at Cordova or Valdez and follows the Copper, Tonsina, Delta and Tanana river valleys. The western route runs from Seward up around Cook Inlet and up to Broad Pass and on into the Interior. Either way, when this project is done there will be high iron from tidewater to Fairbanks."

Mac knew the term "high iron" referred to mainline rail, because it is heavier and thus higher than the lighter rail used for sidings and rail yards. Rail was now made of steel, but the term endured.

Mac set his square jaw contemplatively as he struggled to make sense of the plethora of information Jones had provided. *The government has decided Alaska needs a railroad, and they are going to build it and then run it. They don't know where the line will run, yet they've somehow divined how much it will cost to build. And, the project will be managed by a group of men that for the most part know nothing about Alaska. Still, they have money and need help.*

By evening's end Mac sold his string of pack horses to the government and hired on.

Mac worked side-by-side with the commission crew as they began carving a construction camp out of the Alaskan wilderness. As promised, more men, horses and supplies arrived at Ship Creek and they began building docks, shops, supply terminals, housing and offices.

Most workers arriving at Ship Creek were young men, some chasing dreams and adventure, some escaping the consequences of past adventures. One particularly interesting new arrival, Mac noticed, was a jolly looking fella who always hummed to himself. Curious, he approached the round-faced man and introduced himself. The smiling young man surprised Mac by doing a little jig and bursting in to verse.

> *There'll be strange things done in the midnight sun,*
> *By the folks of the Alaska Rail.*
> *The northern lights will see strange sights,*
> *And someone must tell their tale.*

> *Through calm or turmoil I will share their toil,*
> *And in my lyrical beat,*
> *I'll tell their story be it scandal or glory;*
> *My name is Poetic Pete.*

Mac enjoyed "The Cremation of Sam McGee" and the other verses in "The Spell of the Yukon," but he'd never encountered someone who spoke exclusively in Service-like verse. "Your name is Poetic Pete and you always talk like Robert Service?"

> *When a story needs telling I am always willing,*
> *With the words I find so magical,*
> *To tell the truth, or share a myth,*
> *And make it all a bit lyrical*

> *In my head a verse is dancing, even sets my feet a prancing,*
> *So folks say I'm a bit offbeat.*
> *Cuz when I'm talking, when I'm walking,*
> *I follow that musical beat.*

"Well it's nice to meet you too," said Mac as Poetic Pete danced away. *A bit out of the ordinary, but likeable enough,* he thought.

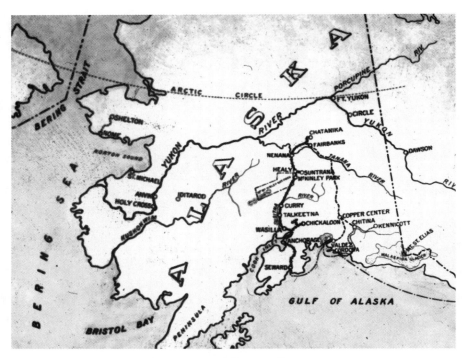

Western and Eastern Routes

Alaska State Library,
Alaska Railroad Tour Lantern Slide Collection, ASL-P198-04

Chapter Two

The Ship Creek camp began as a haphazard collection of white canvas wall tents, horses, men, mud and mosquitoes; then, in calculated steps order was wrested from chaos.

"Line up those crates. Straight rows, always straight rows," said the government engineer. He supervised as the new railroad workers continued to offload and organize the growing stockpiles of supplies and material.

The more time Mac spent with the engineers the more he realized they needed order, structure, in all things. Clutter was unacceptable; chaos had to be subdued. Untamed Alaska needed a railroad and they would provide one.

Mac and his coworkers were perched on a lumber pile enjoying their lunch break when one of the men asked, "Hey Mac, when are we going to start building the damned railroad?"

"The engineers tell me projects like this, like old broncos, tend to be a bit slow out of the chute. But, once they start to feel their oats you'd best hang on tight."

"Let's hope this railroad finds some damned oats real soon. I'm tired of hanging around camp stacking stuff in rows. Always straight rows."

"You'll get a taste of the real Alaska very soon," said Mac. "Summer crew assignments were posted this morning, and while some men will stay here building a more permanent construction camp, most of us will be out in the bush working on the survey crews."

As Mac attempted to clean the accumulation of mud from his boots at day's end he sat down next to his new crew chief. Robert Plumb was a slim man, and the spectacles anchored on his sharp nose gave him an intelligent look. His light brown eyes matched his shirt and hair. It was neatly trimmed and combed, like he'd just stepped out of a San Francisco barber shop. His clothes were clean, except for his mud-caked boots.

"You know it's the high clay content that makes this mud adhere to your boots," Plumb said.

"It's mighty sticky stuff." Mac introduced himself to the engineer, who appeared to be about the same age. "I'll be working on your survey crew this summer."

"Yes. Yes. I requested that you be assigned to me. They say you work hard, have good sense, and know how to work horses. I'm told you are an educated man."

"I am a horse man, but I'm afraid most of my education comes from the lessons of life," answered Mac. Privately, he recalled, *he'd schooled well, but not long. He'd liked the learning but not the schooling so at a young age he'd left school and taken work as a ranch hand. Personal tragedy triggered his escape into the whiskey bottle and the untamed north. Older now, he substituted books for alcohol, education without schooling.* Mac asked, "How about you? You new to this railroad business?"

"New to this government railroad project, but not to railroading. I was working as an engineer and surveyor for the Southern Pacific in California. But that was just a job, and building a railroad across Alaska is a once-in-a-lifetime opportunity for an engineer like me. Reputations will be made. Careers will be launched."

"This is a land of opportunity," said Mac, "though sometimes a bit rough too."

Plumb beamed. "There will certainly be challenges when building a rail line over mountains, across rivers, and over permafrost. But they are all solvable problems, every one of them, just takes good engineering."

I like this man's confidence, thought Mac. The engineer pulled a special case from his vest pocket and removed a glistening oversized round object from the case. "That's a fine looking timepiece," said Mac.

"Oh no! This isn't a watch. This is a Halden Calculex."

"I don't know what that is," said Mac, looking closely at the device.

"A circular slide rule, a calculating machine. With my help, it does complex mathematical calculations."

"I'm sure calculations are important to you engineers."

"Critically important. This whole project will be driven by mathematical calculations: acres to be cleared, board feet of timber to be cut, rail curvature and grade, just to name a few."

And calculations on how much to pay all of us workers, I hope, thought Mac.

"And, there will be many bridges, each with its own complex design, supported by many complex calculations."

"Sounds like we'd better hope that calculating machine doesn't make mistakes," said Mac.

"The machine won't make mistakes," said the engineer, the look on his face turning from serious to double serious, "but the person operating it may, and the consequences could be catastrophic."

By the time Mac completed his mud scraping he decided the man clearly had a good heart. But, he thought, *Plumb's stuffy and over-educated manner might not set well with the new hires, raw and free-spirited young men who have little respect for rules. Might be a good idea to smear a little normal on this book-head.*

"First crew meeting is tomorrow," said Plumb. He walked carefully to avoid the ever-present mud.

"My name is Robert Plumb and I'll be your Crew Chief for the rest of the summer," he said to the assembled workers.

"Mind if we just call you Bob?" asked Mac.

"Actually most people call me Plumb, or Bob," he said as he carefully placed a map of Alaska on the easel beside him. "Gentlemen, we have a big job. The United States is going to build a railroad across Alaska, from tidewater up to Fairbanks." He picked up a wooden pointer and tapped the map. "As you can see, two routes are being considered. This is a critically important decision, and our work will help make that decision. There are eleven survey parties all together. Several originate here at Ship Creek. Others will start from Seward and other points along the southern Alaska coast and three have been sent to Fairbanks to survey the north end."

Plumb-or-Bob explained that each survey party's job was to explore the terrain, conduct preliminary surveys, and locate a viable rail route. "Trains are heavy. They don't turn well, they don't climb well and they're hard to control when going downhill. The perfect railroad is a straight, level line. Since there are no straight and level routes through these mountains our job is to find a route with the fewest curves and manageable grades. And, we'll also need to find places to cross rivers and streams."

"Our crew will work north of here," he said, "between the Susitna River Valley and Broad Pass. This is a difficult area, but I'm sure none of us came to Alaska looking for easy."

There was a strong murmur of assent when Mac stood up and said, "I think I speak for the whole crew when I tell you we'll damn sure get this job done, and done right."

"I appreciate your enthusiasm and look forward to working with each of you."

"And we look forward to working with you Mr. Plumb-bob."

Railroad Crew with Pack Horses

William B. Spearman Photographs,
UAF-2004-143-1, Archives, University of Alaska Fairbanks

Chapter Three

Summer was at its prime as survey crews set out to delineate a transportation corridor that would forever alter the face of Alaska. After rounding the head of Knik Arm Plumb-bob's crew moved up through the vast Susitna River Valley where they had dramatic views of the giant snow covered peak of Mt. McKinley.

Mac led the way while Plumb-bob and the crew followed close behind, each trailing horses laden with supplies and equipment. Mac rode the bay mare. Since their meeting on the muddy shore the horse had given Mac full credit for her release from shipboard confinement, and seemed determined to repay him with affection and dedicated service.

Saddle time was thinking time for Mac. Today he reflected on his recent good fortune. *The commission is committed to building a railroad across Alaska and also committed to operating that railroad. A government run railroad will be immune to the financial woes suffered by the Tanana Valley and other railroads in Alaska. If we can get this line built, there will be good-paying jobs up here for years to come.*

Camping near the confluence of the Talkeetna and Susitna Rivers, they watched the big waters moil by while Plumb-bob explained that bridges across big rivers like these would be key to the new rail system. "Strong steel bridges across the Mississippi River allowed the westward expansion of U.S. railroads. This route will cross many big rivers and high ravines, but with good designs and good materials they are all bridgeable."

"And good construction crews," said a young man.

And good calculations, thought Mac.

Plumb-bob's crew established its first base camp adjacent to the Indian River, just above its union with the Susitna, near a sweeping bend where the clear water pools and the fish congregated. Their job was to find a viable alignment from the Susitna River Valley up to Broad Pass. "In one roughly twenty-mile section the rail line will need to gain almost one-thousand feet in elevation," Plumb-bob said, "and we have to find a route heavy trains will be able to climb."

They scouted routes on horseback, measured elevation changes, and checked soil conditions. As a possible route was located they cleared enough brush to shoot survey lines and then placed preliminary markers.

"Looks like we have company," said Mac when he spotted three tethered horses as they returned to camp one July evening.

"Good evening gentlemen," a sandy haired man said as the weary crew drifted in, "I'm Lieutenant Mears." He was thin like Plumb-bob.

"Good to see you, Sir," said Plumb-bob.

"We're scouting the rail route north from Ship Creek," said Mears. "Commissioner Riggs is taking the route southward from Fairbanks, and we plan to link up with him up in the Broad Pass area."

"Can you spend the night with us?" asked Plumb-bob.

"We were hoping to," said Mears. "I'm anxious to get more acquainted with you and your crew."

At first, Mac was guarded around the commissioner, but was soon calmed by his winning manner. Mears inquired about the personal aspirations of the men gathered around the fire, and sought their views on the project. He told them he'd worked as a rodman on a Great Northern Railway survey crew before joining the Army.

This guy knows railroading, thought Mac, *and he cares about us railroaders.*

"Smoke?" asked Mears, offering cigars to both Plumb-bob and Mac.

The long day of physical labor had sent the crew to their bedrolls but the three older men stayed by the dying fire, chatting about

Alaska. "Mac, you are obviously very familiar with this country," said Mears. His cigar created a smoke screen that even the voracious Alaskan mosquitoes couldn't penetrate. "What do you see as the biggest obstacle this project faces, besides the weather?"

"Truth is, Sir, the weather up here is entirely tolerable. Winters come early and stay late, but with preparation and the right attitude it's just another season. I've lived through a batch of 'em and still manage to look forward to the next one."

"Sounds like you've been here a long time," said Mears. "Were you born here?"

"No, I was born in Spokane Falls, over on the sunny side of Washington State."

"Spokane Falls! That's where I lived as a kid. My dad was assigned to Fort Spokane back in 1889 and I went to school there until I graduated from Gonzaga Prep. When were you there, Mac?"

"We left when I was young," said Mac. "My dad found work on a ranch, around '87 I think it was."

"So how'd you end up in Alaska?" asked Mears.

"Bit of a long story I'm afraid. But the short of it is that after the love of my life took sick and died I drank my way north and scratched around for gold until I ran out of money. Then I worked for the railroad up in Fairbanks until they ran out of money."

"I understand the power of grief. I lost my father when I was young," said Mears, then he shared the personal tragedy of his father's early death after a fall on the icy steps of their home. As the cigars burned out their friendship flickered to life.

Lieutenant Mears and his assistant moved on the next morning as the crew returned to their work. The rail route grew up through the Indian River Valley. It gained elevation as they worked upstream through the verdant and sometimes constricted gorge. Where the valley was wide enough they kept the proposed rail line safely back away from the river, but where the river abutted the steep canyon slopes they were forced to establish an alignment immediately adjacent to the water. "Having the railroad too close to any river will cause problems someday," said Plumb-bob. "They are always fighting at their banks."

"Is there any alternative?" asked Mac.

"Not really. Railroads always require some maintenance and that will be especially true along these rivers."

They defined a route up through the Indian River Valley to the point where the stream veered eastward but the route had to move west and north, and up. "This is where we earn our pay," said Plumb-bob to the crew. "We need to find a way up this grade."

Plumb-bob studied the data they'd collected and worked his Calculex each day. Finally, late one evening he gathered the crew around him. "We have a route that works. There are some three percent grades, which train crews will cuss as long as this railroad exists, but we will be able to get trains up to the high country."

Survey work on the steep grade was challenging even in good weather. Then the rain came, soaking the ground, the men, and the horses. A rock slide missed the men by a narrow margin, but the mare's right front leg was badly injured by falling debris.

"I can't say for certain but it looks broken," said Plumb-bob. "I'm afraid it's the end of the trail for this poor critter."

"Could be broken, or could just be badly bruised," said Mac. "If I was hurt I'd like to have at least three days to heal up before being put out of my misery."

"I reckon the railroad can spare another bucket or two of oats," said Plumb-bob as he strode away.

The mare moved little during the three days, but as Mac approached the corral on her final day she was standing there, waiting for him.

"Well I'll be damned," he said as he set aside the now unneeded rifle. The mare still favored her bruised leg, but she had a new lease on life.

"I was wrong, Mac," said Plumb-bob when he saw the horse standing. "It might take her a while to completely recover but as long as she can keep up I don't see why you can't keep her with us."

The leg improved each week as the crew pushed on northward. The horse, now called Lucky, walked without a limp as the crew staked out the final mile of their section on a frosty fall day. The deep ravine at Hurricane Gulch would required a giant steel bridge, but the crew had established the link connecting the Susitna Valley to the Nenana River valley and Interior Alaska.

"We did it," said Plumb-bob to his weary crew. "Tomorrow morning we'll break camp and head south." A bottle of illicit whiskey appeared and the chief simply took his leave. "I have paper work to do. You men have a pleasant evening."

The men toasted their success as the jug made its way around the campfire.

"To Plumb-bob the engineer, the best damn crew chief on the railroad," one man offered.

"Hip. Hip. Hooray," all replied

"Here's to all the girls in Seattle. May we meet soon."

"Hip. Hip. Hooray."

"Let's drink to our pay, from the U.S. of A."

"Hip. Hip. Hooray."

"To the cussedest land that I know, from the big dizzy mountains that screen it, to the deep deathlike valleys below..."

"Sit down and shut up Pete!"

"To Mac."

"Alcohol and I ain't a good match," said Mac as he refused the bottle and headed to his tent.

Back at Ship Creek the survey crews were soon busy closing up camp for the winter. "This has been a successful season," said Plumb-bob to Mac as the last of the gear was stowed away. "We have the information we need to prepare our final report to President Wilson."

"I expect there is much to consider," said Mac.

"There is. Besides the survey work, we've examined the condition of the existing Alaska Northern and Tanana Valley lines."

"I could have told them about that railroad," said Mac.

"You did more than your share of work this summer, Mac. I'm really sorry you and the rest of the crew are being laid off, but there is no work for you to do this winter."

"That's the story of my life I'm afraid. At least this time I have some money in my pocket."

When Plumb-bob gathered the crew one last time he said, "You've been a great group. I feel certain the government will proceed with the construction of this railroad, probably as soon as next summer. I can't promise anything but I'd expect that any of you wanting a job on this project will have one. This afternoon the government will settle up your final wages, and there is a steamer leaving for Puget Sound on tomorrow's high tide. There'll be room on board for those who want to go along, though I'm sure they will make you pay for your passage."

"Sounds like Poetic Pete is going to Seattle," one of the men said to Mac as they listened to the now familiar Robert Service imitator.

> *I wanted the job, and I sought it;*
> *building Alaska's new rail.*
> *I wanted the job and I got it;*
> *just surveyed a bold new trail.*
> *Yet somehow it's not what I thought it;*
> *hard work is my downfall.*
> *I like the pay that comes with it,*
> *but I'd prefer not to work at all.*
>
> *I came to get rich – I'd do it in a season;*
> *hired on as a surveyor's extra.*
> *The work was hard – not a damn bit of fun,*
> *but I'm totally hooked on Alaska.*
> *I'll go winter down in Seattle,*
> *where I'll naught but dance and sing.*
> *But my passion for this land is epical,*
> *so I'll be back up in the spring.*
>
> *The railroad in Alaska will be calling,*
> *it'll be drawing me in like a yoke.*
> *Yet it won't be the work I'll be wanting,*

so much as just filling my poke.
I'll return next spring not an amateur,
so I'll no longer seek a real job.
I'll look for a do-nothing sinecure,
with steady pay for a wannabe nabob.

"What the hell is a sin-a-cure?" asked a crewman, as Pete danced off.

"I think it's a job with an important sounding title, good pay, and not much work; like a Vice President."

That evening Mac found Plumb-bob packing his personal belongings for the trip back to Seattle, carefully folding each item. "How long do you expect it will take the folks back east to make a decision on a route for this railroad?" asked Mac.

Plumb-bob kept working. Finally he said, "To my way of thinking the western route is clearly the best alignment, but you can bet community leaders and businessmen will be bending the ears of their favorite politicians trying to swing the decision in their favor. Of course the Seward community favors the western route, which would make their town the southern terminus of the new rail line. I'm told there is a businessman there who owns a lot of land he'd like to sell, and is very adept at manipulating the political system to serve his personal interests."

"So whether we have work next spring depends on the outcome of that process?"

"That's right. But, like I told the crew this morning, I expect construction to begin next summer."

"I trust your judgement," said Mac, "but I won't be wasting my summer wages on steamer tickets. Last I heard there were more than a quarter of a million people living in Seattle and that sounds like nothing but trouble to me. There's a big valley with a beautiful little river running through it not far from here. Think I'll head up there, build a little cabin and settle in for the winter. Might even do a little trapping."

"Since you're staying up here would you mind keeping these books for the winter so I don't have to pack then with me? Read them if you like."

Mac smiled and looked appreciatively at the crate of well-read volumes. *A good winter project. I'll quench my thirst for knowledge to help forget my thirst for whiskey.*

"Could you also do a favor for the railroad?" asked Plumb-bob. "That mare could use some personal attention while that leg heals. The government will provide the feed if you'll keep her with you for the winter?"

Mac smiled again. "Lucky and I will be waiting here for you when you get back in the spring."

"Word of this railroad project is spreading fast," said Plumb-bob as they parted. "I'm afraid there will be too many men waiting for us next spring."

PART TWO
Construction Begins
(1915)

First Camp

Chapter Four

"My butt whistle is froze solid," said Toot as he and Cock-eyed Jake walked backwards into the biting wind sweeping across Ship Creek Landing. Beneath his heavy coat the sturdy young man wore both flannel shirts he'd brought with him on the northbound steamer. His sturdy work pants encapsulated long-handled underwear. He wore good boots and wool socks but his feet were still stone cold. He tucked his hands under his arm pits and said, "I've had chilled bones since we got to Alaska, and now my arse is frosted too."

The long-time friends had crossed the Cascades to Seattle and found work at the bustling port, but talk of a big railroad project in Alaska soon drove them on north. The calendar said it was spring but Alaskan seasons pay scant attention to the rules. Lengthening days and higher sun angles hinted of warmer weather but winter was still in charge.

"You said it'd be spring up here," said Toot. "If this is springtime I sure as hell don't want to be up here come winter."

"Well we didn't come to Alaska to get warm, did we?"

"No. We came to Alaska to get rich, but so far all I got is a frozen back side," said Toot as they trudged toward the makeshift camp. Their temporary home, like others in the growing camp, was a canvas wall tent with a small tin stove and birch sapling sleeping bunks cushioned with spruce boughs. They were capable of surviving the Alaskan wilderness though not yet capable of enjoying it.

Earlier that day they'd climbed the bluff just south of the creek bottom looking for a moose to supplement the dry beans they'd brought from Seattle. They found moose tracks and moose pellets, but no moose. The failed hunt and the lingering cold were now weighing on Toot. "I'd like to high tail it out of here, but I reckon there ain't no son-of-a-bitch stupid enough to give us a free ride back to Seattle."

"Sometimes I think your brain is as cock-eyed as my peeper. You know you can't show your face around Seattle, and besides that we're here to find work. The government men will be back soon to start building this railroad. We'll go back to Seattle someday, after our pockets are full of money and the sheriff has quit looking for you."

Smoke rising from the stove pipe drew the men to an oversized tent where Ship Creek neighbors often gathered. The glowing stove was surrounded by recently-arrived job seekers. Some faced the stove with hands open to coax the cold from their fingers. Others stood back-to-stove. The faces in the man circle were all familiar, but for the tall guy in the fur hat. The red-headed young man extended his hand to the Johnny-come-lately. "My partner here is Jake, and my name is Toot."

The bewildered look on the big man's face asked for an explanation. "My full nickname is Sir Fartsalot, but over time it's been shortened to just plain Toot."

"I'm Mac," the tall man said. "Just plain Mac. Welcome to Alaska."

"Hell sakes, we been up here almost two weeks and I ain't never seen you around before. Seems like we ought to be welcoming you to Alaska."

"Actually, I came north almost fifteen years ago," said Mac.

That explains the hat that used to be a wolf, thought Toot, envying the obvious warmth of the hand-sewn headgear. *Wonder if I could make me some under britches out of wolf fur?* "You must a been a gold miner."

"I worked the gold fields from the Yukon to Nome and up by Fairbanks too, but mostly I worked for the Tanana Valley Railroad."

Toot sucked air and broke wind. "Are there already railroads in Alaska?"

"There are," said Mac, "but most of them are going broke."

"If you've already worked for an Alaskan railroad you'll surely get work on this new government project."

"Actually, I worked for them last summer. When they went back south I built a cabin out in the bush and settled in for the winter."

"Folks in Seattle said they'd be starting work this spring, so we came up to be first in line when they start passing out those good jobs," said Jake. "We're expecting them to show up any day now."

"They should be here soon," said Mac. "That's why I'm here."

Toot smiled now. "Well you can't be setting up your camp until this wind blows itself out. We have an extra bunk in our tent and you're welcome to use it until then."

"I'll accept that offer, but only if you boys will help me eat some of the moose haunch I brought."

"Moose and beans," said Jake and Toot in unison and quickly steered Mac to their tent to begin the cooking.

The trio ate well that evening as the newcomers quizzed Mac about Alaska, the government railroad and their job prospects. By time they finally banked the fire for the night and crawled into their bunks the wind had subsided.

Jake awoke with a start, listening but hearing nothing, silence so deep his thoughts came only in whispers. Snow was falling on Ship Creek Landing he realized, choking out all sound. The fire had burned down while they slept and despite the insulating blanket of fresh snow the pervasive Alaskan cold had penetrated the thin tent walls. With the first morning light he slipped out of bed, carefully placed dry wood on the remaining coals, opened the vent and scurried back to his still warm bedroll. The crackle of the awakening fire soon announced that the little stove was back on the job but the now awake men remained in their bunks waiting for the cold air to retreat. Jake asked, "So tell me Mac, do you really think we'll get jobs on this project?"

"Good chance that you will," said Mac. "Building a railroad across Alaska is a big job and the government will make it even bigger."

Toot held his nose. "What do you mean by that?"

"There's the easy way to do things and there's the government way. Most of 'em are decent folks but all the damn rules and forms make it difficult for them to get any work done."

"The big railroads down south were built by private companies weren't they?" asked Jake.

"They were," said Mac. "Congress decided to have the government build this one to avoid corruption like that associated with the private construction of the transcontinental railroad."

Toot, breathing again, "Corruption?"

"Yep. Railroad executives stole from their own companies, manipulated stock and spent government money influencing the very politicians who were paying them."

Toot grinned knowingly. "So the railroad bosses lined their pockets with government money?"

"Not only theirs, more than thirty congressmen admitted to receiving stock options."

"So do you think a government-built railroad will eliminate the dishonesty?" asked Jake.

"I reckon it'll be a trade off," said Mac. "There will be less corruption, but they'll likely waste a fair amount of time and money."

"Ought to create plenty of work," said Jake.

"That's what I'm thinking," said Mac. "More jobs for us working folks. This government ain't perfect, but they take damn good care of their employees."

"That's the problem," said Jake. "This project will attract too damn many workers. Word of these good jobs is all around Puget Sound."

"You boys from Seattle?"

"Hell no," said Toot "We only stayed in that moss-covered country long enough to rustle up the money to come up here. And don't be asking questions about how we rustled up that money."

Jake jumped in. "We're originally from over Spokane way."

"I was born there too, a few years before you boys. In fact, you men remind me a little of myself when I was your age. Tell you what, I don't know where this railroad project is taking us, but I'll do whatever I can to help you young fellas get work."

"You'd do that for us?"

"That's a promise."

"We surely appreciate that." Jake got up and put a kettle of water on the now hot stove. When the water boiled he added coffee and his tin cup was soon filled with the steaming hot brew. The sharp aroma filled the tent, enticing the other two to leave their bedrolls and fortify their souls with thick camp stove coffee.

"First thing I have to do today is tend my horse," said Mac, clutching the hot cup between his large hands.

"I see a government brand on that horse," said Jake.

"She belongs to the railroad. She hurt her leg last fall and I've been nursing her all winter. She's good as new."

"You get that horse taken care of, and when the snow stops we'll help you set up your camp."

"I'd welcome the help," said Mac. He put the fur hat back atop his head. "I plan to stick around here and greet those government men when they step off the boat."

Ship Creek Tent City

FIC photographs; Anchorage Museum,
B1979.001.85

Chapter Five

The Alaskan spring is an elusive temptress, promising relief to her winter-weary residents by adding six minutes of sunshine to each new day but delivering warmth with agonizing slowness. Finally, as though weary of the process, she unleashes the break-up and the snow becomes water and the land becomes mud. The young men waiting at Ship Creek in 1915 welcomed the change with bright faces and soaring spirits. They left tent flaps open and hung bedding out in the fresh spring breeze.

When retreating inlet ice allowed the Alaska Engineering Commission men to return to Ship Creek Mac was there waiting for them. "How are you and that horse doing?" Plumb-bob asked.

"We both wintered well, thank you."

"That's good, because President Wilson has given us the go-ahead on this project. The main line will follow the western route, running 473 miles from Seward to Fairbanks, and there will be a branch line to the Matanuska coal fields."

"The Alaska Northern already has a line running north from Seward," said Mac, "up to the head of Turnagain Arm."

"The President also authorized the purchase of that line," said Plumb-bob. "It'll be incorporated into the new government railroad."

That's music to my ears, thought Mac, and then caught himself. *I'm starting to think like that crazy poetry guy.* The verbalization of his thought became a simple, "That's good news."

"Sure is, but what we need to do right now is offload the material we brought up with us. You ready to get to work?"

"That's why I'm here," said Mac, looking at the other men getting off the just-arrived vessel. "Is Lieutenant Mears with you?"

Plumb-bob nodded knowingly. "He'll be leaving Seattle on April 19th."

The coastal community of Seward is often shadowed by a thick cloud cover and when Lieutenant Frederick Mears arrived in the spring of 1915 another cloud loomed: John Ballaine.

"Seward is honored to be designated as the southern terminus of the new government railroad," said Ballaine, standing conspicuously at the front of the local crowd welcoming Mears to their town. The businessman had been the impetus behind the Alaska Northern Railroad, with plans to build a rail line all the way to Fairbanks. But, they had only built seventy-two miles of main line rail, and they were out of money.

"It's good to be here in Seward," said Mears. "We're anxious to get this railroad project started. Of course one of the first things to do is complete the purchase of the Alaska Northern."

Ballaine had lobbied hard to influence the government's decision to purchase his failing rail line, and the selection of Seward as the southern terminus of the government railroad promised great demand for his considerable real estate holdings in that town. "Our company, and our community, stand ready to help."

"I'll take you at your word," said Mears, "even though your newspaper's criticism of the railroad's hiring policy wasn't very helpful."

"Well I don't have much to say about what they print," said the man who owned the paper, unconvincingly.

I'll need to be wary of this man, thought Mears as he excused himself and moved away to greet other Seward residents. Anxious to get to work, he completed his Seward duties in short order and was soon on his way to Ship Creek.

Mears, a career Army officer, served as General Superintendent and Chief Engineer of the Panama Railroad Company prior to his appointment to the Alaska Engineering Commission. The appointment ruffled the bureaucratic feathers of the Army Corps of Engineers because Mears was a cavalry officer and not a Corps of Engineers officer, but special Congressional action confirming his assignment to the Commission quickly ended the spat.

Mac was pleased to see the six-foot man in the pointed hat striding across the muddy encampment, his pants tucked tightly in the tops of his high lace-up work boots. "Welcome back Mr. Mears. Sounds like we're ready to build a railroad."

"Good to see you," said Mears. "At least we're ready to get ready to build a railroad. I have business to tend to right now, but if you have time this evening stop by my place and we'll smoke a cigar."

"Been a lot of changes here," said Mac as he sat in the comfortable wood-framed canvas chair in front of Mears' temporary quarters. The small campfire trimmed the edges from the evening chill and set the mood for relaxed conversation. "Was lonely here by the creek a year ago, and now it's getting hard to find a place to pitch a tent."

Mears handed Mac a fine Philippine cigar. "And this is just the beginning. This railroad will bring dramatic change to this creek bottom and a big swath of this Territory. I hope you Alaskans are ready for it."

"I'm damn happy to see this project get started."

"That's good, because we're moving full speed ahead now. Chairman Bill Edes is responsible for general supervision of all Commission activities, with his headquarters down in Seward. Commissioner Tom Riggs is tasked with completing the location work. I'm in charge of building the new rail line, and I'm setting up our construction camp here at Ship Creek."

"The headquarters is at Seward but the construction camp is here at Ship Creek?" asked Mac.

"The Alaska Northern offices in Seward provide a readily available headquarters facility for Chairman Edes, but I wanted a more central location for the construction camp. There is plenty of room to store material along the creek, we can build the rail line both directions from here and this port is closest to the Matanuska coal fields."

"The tides and ice here will be a challenge," said Mac.

"You're right about that. The Seward port is ice-free all winter, but the Alaska Northern is in such bad shape that until the line is refurbished we'll have no way to get supplies and equipment up here where it's needed."

"I'm told that line needs some serious fixing," said Mac.

"The promoters were very optimistic when they started as the Alaska Central, but since they never made enough money to even pay their operating expenses there was no money for maintenance."

Mac stared into the fire for a time, smoking his cigar, then asked, "But the government thinks that even though these other railroads are failing they'll be able to make this one successful?"

"The government has a broader role Mac, so their definition of success is different from that of a private company. After listening to the debate they've determined that Alaska needs a railroad. President Wilson said in his State of the Union speech that Alaska is a storehouse that should be unlocked, and according to him the key is a system of railways. And, Alaska's delegate to Congress, Jim Wickersham, has plenty of influence and he has pushed hard to get this railroad authorized by congress."

"So apparently the government knows they'll be supporting the railroad for some time."

"Congress surely knows the rail lines up here have struggled financially, so they must anticipate that this one will need their help, at least to get started. But, our job is real clear. We have the opportunity to build a railroad through a land unlike any other."

"This is a spectacular place," said Mac. "Giant mountains surrounded by grand valleys that are drained by untamed rivers. Beautiful, but not an easy place to build a railroad."

Mears nodded his head. "The Panama project was an unprecedented engineering challenge too, with difficult terrain in a harsh climate, but we got it done. And, it too was a government project so we were also faced with the inefficiencies inherent in the bureaucratic process and the disjointed leadership inherent in the political process."

"Sounds like you know what you're up against."

"The bureaucrats are mostly just annoying, but the politicians can be downright nasty, not to mention illogical and unethical," said Mears. "In this position it will be hard to avoid getting crosswise with some of the political players. In fact, that fella in Seward already has me concerned."

"I've heard of him," said Mac.

"I'll handle him, and others like him. This is an important project Mac. Just as the Panama Canal redefined interoceanic transportation this railroad will redefine Alaskan transportation. I'm confident that with a little patience and the help of good men like you we'll get this railroad built."

"Well I'm looking forward to the challenge, and grateful for the work. I expect you'll be hiring a lot of workers real soon then."

Mears looked at the large and worrisome camp spreading along the creek, canvas tents full of unharnessed energy. "We will, but we already have more men here than we can hire."

Waiting for the Mail

Pyatt-Laurence Collection; Anchorage Museum,
B1983.146.313

Chapter Six

"It's just supply and demand," Toot said. "We're demanding work but the railroad ain't supplying any." Mac and others who had worked the prior summer were rehired but it was a waiting game for Cock-eyed Jake and Toot. This evening the near broke and obviously frustrated men had dropped by their friend Mac's tent.

Mac cleared a place for the men to sit. "They should be hiring real soon. Be patient and be ready to pitch in as soon as they need help."

"How much are we gonna get paid Mac?" Toot asked, sitting straight-backed on the edge of the bunk.

"The general labor rate is thirty-seven and a half cents an hour. Carpenters and other skilled workers will get even more."

"Decent wages," said Jake. "At that rate we could make over seven hundred dollars a year."

Mac swatted an early season mosquito that had followed his friends into the tent. "We won't be as rich as the boss men. I heard today that each member of the Alaska Engineering Commission gets paid ten thousand dollars a year."

Toot's face lit up. "Well if they've got bosses they are sure as hell going to need people to boss."

"They'll need construction workers when they start building the rail line," said Mac. "But first they have to build the construction camp here at Ship Creek. As soon as the materials get here they'll be needing more carpenters. They brought some with them from Seattle but they'll likely need more."

"How can we get railroad carpenter jobs?" asked Toot.

"What you need to do is get some carpenter experience real fast. Go hang around where they are building that big warehouse, watch what the carpenters do and learn the jargon."

Toot smiled and nodded. "I can do that."

Jake sat quietly, a frown forming on his face. "I don't think carpentering in the job for me. I can do the figuring just fine but it's hard to saw straight lines with this independent thinking eye of mine."

"They'll need some survey helpers this summer too."

Jake hesitated again. "Surveying may not be my calling either."

"Don't you worry Jake, we'll find work for you," said Mac.

Job-seeker's demands for information prompted the railroad to issue a written notice addressing the job situation. Rumors ran amok at the Ship Creek camp and real news drew a crowd. The curious would-be workers stood around the posted notice, reading, mumbling and scratching their heads. "Sounds like something written by the lawyers. Sure do wish someone would explain what they are really trying to tell us," said one of the out-of-work men.

Another stepped forward from the crowd. "My unfortunate experience in court proceedings forced me to listen to way too much lawyer talk. Let me translate this for you fellas."

"*The following notice has been prepared to serve as a means of giving reliable information to those making inquiries in regard to the work at Ship Creek, Knik Arm, Alaska.* Means we're from the Government, you can trust us!" The crowd laughed, then cheered, then grew silent in anticipation of further explanation from the expert.

"*There will be very few positions to offer to men on a salary or daily wage basis on the construction work at Ship Creek, Alaska.* Means they think they can build this railroad without any hired help.

A limited number of railroad station men, experienced in the work of clearing right-of-way, culvert building and railroad grading may find work at or near Ship Creek, Knik Arm, on the terms offered by railroad contractors. Means there may be some work for experienced railroad builders, but their rules are more important than your experience.

Gangs will commence clearing about May 1ˢᵗ and grading about May 15ᵗʰ or June 1ˢᵗ." Means they ain't sure when they'll get started.

There will be work at Ship Creek for a very limited number of experienced carpenters and carpenter helpers (having their own tools) in the erection of docksheds, buildings, living quarters and storehouses, as soon as the necessary material has been assembled. Means they'll need carpenters. You bring the tools and they'll bring the lumber, but the lumber ain't here yet.

The carpenters and carpenter helpers will be paid on an hourly basis and charged for their board at the rate of $1.00 per day. Means they'll pay you to build living quarters, and then charge you a buck a day to live in the quarters you just built.

The Commission will <u>not</u> engage large numbers of men on force account basis, and those going to Ship Creek, Alaska, with the idea of finding ready employment on the new work will be largely disappointed. Means finding work on this project might not be as easy as we were told."

"I still ain't sure what a force account basis or railroad station men means?" asked one of the men.

"Station men are contractors who do a certain piece of work and get paid when they get it done right. Those working on a force account basis work under the direction of the Commission and never miss a payday, regardless of what they've accomplished."

Back in the privacy of their tent Jake and Toot plotted their future. "How are you planning to get yourself hired?" Jake asked. "You have no carpenter experience and no tools."

"Getting a little experience and some old tools won't be a problem for the Tooter. That poetry fella got a railroad job and I'm sure as hell going to get one too."

"Yeah, I hear him."

HIGH IRON TO FAIRBANKS

Was just doing my jig when they offered me a gig,
That is too good to be true.
Each and every day I'll draw my pay,
But there'll be no work to do.

Won't break my breakin' my back out buildin' track,
Instead I'll be a deskman.
The railroad hired me, gonna pay me,
To be their song and dance man.

"The railroad hired Poetic Pete to sing and dance?" asked Jake.
"Yeah, sort of."
"So exactly what is Pete's new job?"
"He's the new CFI."
"What the hell does CFI mean?"
"Probably means that he's a Complete Idiot of some kind."

The White City

Chapter Seven

"I got us a plan," Toot announced to his partner as they moseyed along the muddy path meandering through the maze of canvas dwellings.

"Seems like it was your plan that got us up here to Alaska," replied the now skeptical Cock-eyed Jake, "and that hasn't worked out so good. Neither one of has a job yet."

"We got to be patient. Mac is looking out for us and they're hiring a few more men every day."

"Yeah, they gave a good job to that song and dance guy, but you and I still don't have work."

"Mac already told us this railroad doesn't always make sense. Now do you want to hear about my plan?"

"I expect I'm gonna get told whether I want to hear it or not."

"Here's my idea. Men are arriving in this camp every week and they all need a place to stay, so we should build a bunkhouse and rent out sleeping space. That way we'll be making some money while we're waiting for work."

"How are we going to build a bunkhouse?" asked Jake. "I know you got yourself some rusty tools, but we don't have any lumber."

"Every day I hang around with those railroad crews, learning about carpentering, and one thing I've learned is they waste a lot of lumber. They let me clean up their scraps for fire wood and some of those scraps are good lumber, just in small pieces. I can gather up enough short boards to lay a wood floor. We can cut birch trees for floor joists -- that's what carpenters call the beams that hold up the floor. Then we'll nail the lumber scraps to the birch joists and we'll have a floor. Won't be real pretty but it'll be dry."

"I'm following you so far partner but we're going to need more than just a floor."

"Well you ain't heard the whole plan yet! We can build short sidewalls the same way as the floor, with birch framing and scrap lumber for siding. Then we'll frame up the rest of the walls and ceiling with more birch and cover it with canvas."

"And where are we going to get the canvas?" asked Jake.

"Buy it."

"Buy it! "We barely have enough money left to buy food and you want to buy canvas with it."

"This is business, Jake. We're going to have to invest a little money to get started but we'll get it back after we're open for business. Besides, I know where I can get us a special deal on some canvas that has been used a little bit."

"This worries the hell out of me, but you're starting to make sense."

"Of course I'm making sense. We'll become experienced carpenters by building our own bunkhouse, and then we'll make some money renting out bunks."

"Earnings and profit are words I like to hear," said Jake, "but you didn't mention things like debt, bills and insolvency."

"We ain't getting in this race to lose."

"You might be right, partner. My dad was in business for a time. It was hard work, long days and customers who couldn't or wouldn't pay, but he came home happy because he was his own boss. Seems like a risk worth taking. Let's give it a try."

Toot's architectural design was as sound as his borrowed carpenter skills and the canvas-covered creation went up so fast that even the real carpenters were impressed. The scrap-lumber-over-birch floor provided a dry if not level surface. Cock-eyed Jake didn't notice and Toot said it would allow for drainage should the canvas roof spring a leak. The side walls were unsightly but functional and the birch saplings braced with leftover lumber provided a sturdy frame for the canvas cover. When a wooden door was hung on hinges made from scrap leather the bunkhouse was enclosed. "How many bunks you think we can put in this place?" asked Jake. They stood admiring the nearly finished structure.

"A bunch. They'll be about four feet square and eight feet deep. That'll give each man a couple extra feet at the bottom of his bunk to store his duffel bag and extra underwear."

"Sounds more like a chicken coop than a bunkhouse."

"Kind of the same idea, except chickens don't pay rent and our compartments are bigger."

"Not much bigger."

"These guys are eventually going to be working," said Toot. "All they want is a place to sleep. They call 'em muzzle loaders."

An additional bunk was added on top of each stack, tucked tightly beneath the peak of the canvas ceiling. The top bunk strengthened the rack of bunks and provided bracing for the birch sapling rafters supporting the roof. A crude ladder provided access to this penthouse level of the eighteen-bunk facility. Less than a week after Toot had his original epiphany the bunkhouse was ready for occupants.

"We can charge a buck a day for each bunk," said Jake. "That's what the railroad is charging people to stay in their dormitory."

"Their building is made of real boards and their floor doesn't lean toward the creek. How about we just charge six bits a day?"

"Okay," said Jake. The partners hung a hand-painted sign above the door and the Bunkhouse Royale was open for business.

Material Yard at Ship Creek

Sydney Laurence, Alaska Railroad Collection; Anchorage Museum,
B1979.002.AEC.L12a

Chapter Eight

"The foreman says the lumber supply finally got ahead of the carpenter supply, and he sent me here to get signed on as a railroad carpenter," Toot said to the diminutive man sitting straight-backed behind the large wooden table. The conspicuously displayed nameplate proclaimed that he was Nigel LeCount, Supervisor of Accounts. The bespectacled man in the clean white shirt was dedicated to the premise that rules must be followed, records must be accurate and not a single penny could be spent until approved by the Supervisor of Accounts. According to the Commission's organization chart the engineers were in charge of the project but they could do little without his approval. The engineers had the authority but Nigel had the power.

"And you are?" Nigel asked the young man sitting before his table-desk.

"Toot. Two 'o's' with a 't' on each end."

Nigel did not smile. "The United States Government requires your real name."

"That would be DeeWayne, with a double 'e' and capital 'w.'"

Nigel, the product of his mother's British formality stirred in with his father's French arrogance, had little sympathy for the plight of others. He carefully reviewed the form the man had just presented to him.

"So Mr. DeeWayne with a double 'e' and a capital 'w,' I see we are hiring you as a Carpenter's Helper. Do you possibly have carpenter experience?"

"Yep."

"How much?"

"Plenty. Just finished building a bunkhouse."

"Do you own your own tools?"

"Same ones I used to build that bunkhouse."

"Precisely how many tools do you own?"

"Never bothered to count 'em. Your notice says I need experience and tools, but it don't say a damn thing about how much or how many."

Nigel stood, smoothed his sharply parted hair and carefully moved toward a group of meticulously arranged wooden boxes. Government forms were in one area, records in another, and office supplies in yet another. "The railroad's notice does not specify how much experience or how many tools are needed," he said, carefully removing a piece of paper from the box neatly labeled as FORMS. "But we do need real carpenters. Is there anything that actually qualifies you to be a Carpenter's Helper?"

"Sure is, the carpenter foreman's signature on this piece of paper. And, I'm wondering, is there anything that qualifies you to be an asshole?"

Nigel was speechless as he looked at the properly signed form. "Your paperwork is in order Mr. DeeWayne so you will be hired, but if you fail to meet the railroad's performance standards you shall be terminated."

"I ain't here to meet your standards mister Little Count, I'm here to raise your standards."

Nigel sat down behind his table-desk, sniffed the air with a frown, methodically inserted the buff-colored form in the typing machine and began striking the keys in perfect cadence.

Ship Creek Alaska 1915

Pyatt-Laurence Collection; Anchorage Museum,
B1983.146.21

Chapter Nine

There were one hundred men on the railroad payroll by the end of May but Cock-eyed Jake wasn't one of them.

"I've talked to every foreman on the property and they tell me they'll be needing men, but my name never comes up when they actually hire folks," he said to Toot one evening. The two men sat on the hillside south of the creek bottom enjoying the much improved though not-quite-yet-summer weather.

"Let's face it, Jake. The railroad probably ain't ever going to hire you. Most folks figure if you can't see straight you can't think straight either, and I sure as hell understand the problem. Being known as Sir Fartsalot doesn't open doors for me either. But, I've learned that you can miss out on a lot of opportunities sitting around worrying about what's not right in this world. Best to just let the fools underestimate your abilities, then show them what you can do."

Jake sat quietly for some time, watching the never-ending commotion down along the creek. "You're probably right. At least I have this little business of ours to work on, and now that the bunks are filled up we're taking in twelve dollars a day. That's some good money."

"That's damn good money, partner. This might be one of those times when life is trying to teach us a lesson and maybe we ought to pay attention for once. Looks to me like the folks who are going to make the real money off this railroad project ain't going to be the workers; it's going to be those who are selling stuff to the workers and to the railroad. The railroad is planning to set up a regular town on the bluff up behind here this summer and I think we could make some money if we had a business in that new town."

"What kind of business do you have in mind?"

"Since this canvas bunkhouse is working out good for us," said Toot, "why don't we buy a lot in this new government town and build a real bunkhouse."

"I like your idea, but it'll take money to get started and we don't have a bunch of extra cash stashed away just yet. That's why I still need to get a job."

"You could become a station man," said Toot. "That way you could make good money without having to get hired by the railroad."

"I've heard talk of this station man thing, but I'm still not sure what it means."

"They say the railroad plans to hire small groups of workers to do certain jobs, like clear brush."

"I'd still have to get hired."

"Not exactly. The railroad will issue a contract to a group of workers and they'll pay you when the work is done."

"So we'd get paid for what we do and not for how we look."

"Or where you look. As long as you get the brush cleared I don't think they'd give a whoopty damn which way that eye points," said Toot. He grinned wide.

"Let's go find Mac. He'll know exactly how this station man system works."

Jake listened attentively while Mac explained. "The Commission plans to station out much of the construction work, following the system used to build railroads in the Western United States. This system works well when they have tasks that the engineers can define in specific units. Clearing trees and brush can be described by the number of acres to be cleared, and grading can be shown as cubic yards of material to be moved."

"So why aren't they called clearing men and grading men?"

"The railroad right-of-way is measured out in one hundred foot units," said Mac, "and numbered station markers define the beginning and ending of each unit."

"So the distance from station four hundred to station five hundred would be ten thousand feet?"

"That's right," said Mac. "Plumb-bob and those other railroad engineers can calculate the number of acres that need to be cleared between defined stations and contract to have that work done at a specific price per acre."

Jake's face lit up. "I can help build this railroad by working as a private contractor."

Mac's supportive look required no words.

"Then I'm going to be a station man," said Jake. "Do you two want to join me?"

"I think you'll do just fine in the contracting business, but I plan to stay up here in Alaska, hopefully working for this railroad," said Mac. "I can't give up my railroad job, even if it is only seasonal work."

"I'm not sure I want to stay in Alaska forever," said Toot, "but I'm sticking with this carpentering job for a while yet. I'm learning the trade, I like the crew I'm working with, the pay is good and my boss usually ain't too bossy. Besides that, I'm getting us all the free lumber we need to keep the Bunkhouse Royale fixed up."

Mac followed Jake and Toot as they walked out through the tent door. "Just because I can't join your station man business doesn't mean we can't be business partners. I've been thinking that the three of us should start a business in this new railroad town. We could buy a lot with the money I saved last summer, build a business and watch it grow right along with the town."

Toot looked at Jake then turned to Mac. "We were just talking about the same damn thing. We're thinking that a more permanent version of the Bunkhouse Royale would do very well here."

"A businesslike version of that lopsided tent-hotel has real potential. Sounds like we have some planning to do, partners."

"While we're working on that plan," said Jake, "I'm going to get my station man business put together. I think I know where I can find some men to work with me."

First Tracks

Chapter Ten

Many Ship Creek residents were European immigrants who had helped build railroads across America. Their names spoke of many cultures and our language was foreign to them but their backs were strong and their hearts pure. Some lived at the Bunkhouse Royale, where Jake found them lounging in their bunks. *Alone with their private dreams*, he thought, *conversations that require no translation*. He said, "I'm looking for some good men to partner up with me and get a railroad building contract. We'll be what they call station men. The work will be hard and the living conditions will be difficult but the pay will be good and we'll work for ourselves."

After a discussion in a medley of languages the men responded.

"I was born with the shovel in me hands," said Paddy from Ireland.

Kosta the Greek, Oleg the Russian and Hans the German answered wordlessly, heads bobbling.

"Yah, and I can swing da ax, you bettcha," said Sven from Norway, "but da English not goot."

"I'll do the talking and the paper work," said Jake. "You men just need to sign your name and do your work. If they ask any questions I'll look them in the eye and swear that we're all good Americans."

Five faces lit up.

"Welcome partner," said Jake as he shook hands with each man. "You are all strong and enthusiastic. Tomorrow I'll find out how to get a station man contract."

At the tent-office marked "Contracting," Jake learned he would have to submit a proposal for station work to compete for brush clearing work.

"If you and your partners are selected," the clerk said, "you will be required to cut down all trees, logs and brush in the right-of-way to within eighteen inches of the ground. You must then remove or burn the logs and slash unless a railroad engineer directs you to save the logs. You'll be paid for each acre cleared."

"Seems fair enough to me," said Jake.

"The railroad will furnish the tools and supplies you need," the clerk said, "at a very reasonable price. The railroad will also provide horses and harnesses for $3 per day, and that includes the feed."

"Feed for the horses or feed for the men?" asked Jake.

"Just for the horses, unless you like to eat oats."

"My partners are all experienced railroad builders, but we don't know much about contracting. Can you tell me how to figure out what price to charge for the work?"

"The railroad expects to pay from thirty to seventy-five dollars per acre for clearing work, depending on the density and character of the timber to be removed. My advice is to inspect the work sites, and then prepare your bid based on how much work you will need to do in the specific area. Make it high enough to pay you and your partners a reasonable wage, but of course you need to be competitive."

"That's exactly what we'll do," said Jake, looking up at the clerk, and down at the proposals lying on the clerk's desk.

Back at the Bunkhouse Royale Jake explained the process to his new partners. Finally, Sven said, "You should yust wisit dem sites and count da trees and den ve vill make da bid."

"Aye," said Paddy.

"Ne," said Kosta.

"Da," said Oleg.

"Ja," said Hans.

"This will be an easy day for you," said Jake as he swung up on the rented saddle horse. Following the rail line north and east from Ship Creek through the spring greenery exploding between the Chugach Mountains and Knik Arm he reflected. *This cussed country bamboozles me. A few weeks ago her forever frozen look made me want to run like hell, but now the same goddamn place makes me want to stay forever.*

He took careful notes throughout the day while examining station markers, terrain and thickness of the timber. That evening Jake reported back to his partners. "Some sites are over two miles long. Others are shorter but they have more trees and brush to be removed. I'd suggest we submit a bid of fifty dollars per acre to clear the right-of-way on a site between stations 3770 and 3820. At that rate we should get the bid and still make good money."

"How much might them other bouzzies be biddin?" asked Paddy.

"I have a suspicion that our bid will have a good chance of winning."

"Aye, ne, da, ja!" the men said in turn.

"Vill dey vant to see citizen papers," asked Sven?

"We won't have to show any papers, but we will all have to sign the proposal. When we get to the Contracting office in the morning you boys just sign on the line where I sign and let me do all the talking."

"Aye, yah sure, ne, da, ja!"

The helpful clerk reviewed the document Jake submitted the following morning. "This looks complete. You boys just need to sign on the bottom and it will all be official."

Jake signed conspicuously and chatted with the clerk while Paddy, Sven, Kosta, Oleg and finally Hans quietly signed the document. "Thanks again for helping us," said Jake as they prepared to leave. "You pick us and we will do a good job for you."

The men silently followed Jake back to the drafty bunkhouse to await the outcome of the railroad's selection process. For Jake, the persuasiveness he'd used on others became self-doubt when talking to himself. A group of good men trusted him, followed him into a new venture, raised their hopes, and now he had to deliver.

Station Man Camp

P.S. Hunt, Alaska Railroad Collection; Anchorage Museum,
B1979.002.AEC.G659

Chapter Eleven

"The first station man contracts will be awarded this week," the clerk told Jake when he visited the Contracting tent first thing Monday morning. "Keep checking back."

On Tuesday Jake got a quick, "no awards yet," when he dropped by the now familiar tent-office.

Jake sensed bad news when the clerk was slow to answer on Wednesday. "Contract No. 1 went to David and Robertson, with a crew of 30 men."

"We have to be patient," said Jake to his partners back at the Bunkhouse, trying hard to appear more confident than he really was.

On Thursday contracts No. 2 through No. 6 were awarded to other partnerships.

The first contracts on Friday morning went to crews headed by J. Merrick and A. Moen. Finally, a contract was awarded to Jake's crew for fifty dollars per acre. The partnership, called the Damn Yankees, was in business!

"Hooz going to pay for dis stuff?" asked Sven as the newly formed partnership packed tools, camp supplies and food on rented railroad horses. The station man crews were mobilizing, anxious to get to work and anxious to get paid. The saws, axes and other tools came from the railroad supply depot while the dried beans and other food items were requisitioned from the railroad commissary.

"Don't worry. Nigel LeCount has a tent full of clerks keeping records and they'll deduct the cost of this stuff when they settle up with us," said Jake. "No money comes out of our pocket yet."

"Dat's good."

"And they're giving it to us at a fair price," said Jake.

"Yah sure."

The Damn Yankees, like other station man crews, were equal partners and when the work was done each would get an equal share of the pay. Among the equals the leadership role fell to Jake because he could speak English and because he could speak engineer.

"This will be our temporary home," Jake said as they set up their camp along a small stream near station marker 3770, the beginning point of their job site.

The partners were already hard at work when a serious-looking man arrived on horseback. "I'm Robert Plumb, the railroad engineer who will be inspecting your work, sometimes called Plumb-bob."

"I'm Jake, sometimes called Cock-eyed Jake. These are my partners."

Jake could not decipher the look on the engineer's face, but the way he studied his crew was worrisome.

"How long have you known these men?" asked Plumb-bob.

"A short while," said Jake.

"Do they know how to work?"

"I think so. They've had hard times recently, but that doesn't make them lazy."

"Well I need to warn you; future contracts will go to the crews that get the job done. Those who don't perform will not be rehired."

"We'll do our best sir."

Plumb-bob carefully marked the area to be cleared, and with his work efficiently complete prepared to move on. "I'll be back in a few days to see how these men are doing," he said as he rode away.

As the crew returned to work Sven asked, "Ve hav to cut da trees da government vay, but do ve have to follow da government clock?"

"We're contractors, so we can work as long as we want to," said Jake. "The sooner we're done the sooner we get paid."

"Yah, ve should not let da daytime be vasting."

Jake's partners spoke sparingly but worked tirelessly. Sven was a skilled woodsman with a lean build and sinewy muscles. Oleg was short and stout like the horses he handled with proficiency. With machine-like stamina the always smiling Paddy single handedly worked one end of the large whip saw while the others took turns on the opposite end. Kosta, Hans and Jake eagerly and instinctively tackled whatever tasks needed doing. With the Damn Yankees on the attack the trees and brush were soon in full retreat.

"You men have accomplished more than I expected," said Plumb-bob when he returned later in the week. He vigilantly inspected the site, made numerous precise calculations with his Calculex and scribbled in his notebook. "Very good." He reviewed his numbers. "Very good work indeed."

"Thank you," said Jake while his partners looked on.

"Let me remind you," said Plumb-bob, "that the railroad wants to save all large diameter trees to use as ties or bridge timbers."

"What exactly is a large diameter tree?" asked Jake.

"It is one that exceeds the specified width and height criteria. The width," he said while holding his hands side-to-side, "is the horizontal measurement." Pointing toward the top of a nearby tree he said, "The height is the vertical measurement from the ground to the top of the large diameter segment of the tree."

With a mischievous glint in his glacier-blue eyes Sven said, "but ve can't reach to da top of dat tree to measure da height."

"You can measure the tree after you fall it."

"On da ground ve measure sidevays to know da height?" asked Sven, repeating the engineer's side-to-side hand gesture.

"That would be correct."

"And on da ground da wertical measure is da vidth of da tree?"

"Yes, I...I...I suppose so," said Plumb-bob as he became the one struggling to extract meaning from words.

"So to know da height ve measure da vidth and to know da vidth ve measure da height?" Sven chuckled.

The other partners laughed out loud, but none laughed as loud as Plumb-bob.

"This is a fine crew," Plumb-bob told Jake as he prepared to leave, "one of the best I've seen."

With the railroad man gone the men gathered around Jake. "Plumb-bob told me we can expand our crew if we want, but I don't see any reason to. This group can get the work done, and more partners would just mean less pay for each of us."

"Aye, ne, da, ja!"

"Yah, and vhen do ve get paid?"

"After the work is done Plumb-bob will give us a piece of paper certifying that we've completed our contract, and describing exactly how many acres we cleared. When the paper is approved by Nigel they'll pay us."

"So ve vill have only one pay day?"

"Yeah, only one pay day for each contract, but it'll be a good one."

"Do ve get more work den?"

"Plumb-bob said the railroad will continue to station out work so we should have brush clearing contracts until freeze-up, if he continues to be happy with us. But, we can bid on other types of work if we're interested. The Commission is putting out station man contracts for things like building wagon roads, laying water lines, painting, supplying railroad ties, even for supplying hay."

Jake studied the silent faces. "We like this brush clearing work and were making good money so seems to me we should just keep doing what we're good at."

"Yah, da bird in one hand is better den two fish in dat tree."

Townsite Area Above Ship Creek

Pyatt-Laurence Collection; Anchorage Museum,
B1983.146.274

Chapter Twelve

The temporary community erupting along Ship Creek soon had over two thousand residents, accompanied by boarding houses, a variety of stores, and even a newspaper. Because the railroad needed the limited creek bottom space for rail yards, administration buildings and support facilities the Commission decided to develop a new town site on the plateau just south of the creek bottom.

"Steep—Damn—Hill," Jake said between breaths as he, Toot and Mac powered themselves up the road connecting Ship Creek to the new town site with the oxygen rich sea level air. The partner's plan to invest in the new town was now sustained by their steady income and the men were using their weekend rest day to explore potential business sites.

From atop the hill the Chugach Mountains rose to the east. Below, the hypnotic Cook Inlet waters swirled as though unsure which way to go next, and across the water Mount Susitna slumbered. Further north the glistening snow covered peak of Mount McKinley reached high into the summer sky.

"There is post card scenery no matter which direction I look," said Jake, "a dandy place for a new city."

Toot slowly turned a complete circle. "A beautiful spot it is. They say the railroad is already surveying a hundred and sixty acres for the town site, so they must expect this place to keep growing. I think this will become the biggest city in all of Alaska before long."

"Could be," said Mac, "but that won't likely happen if they stick with this crazy idea of leasing lots instead of selling them. They can't expect folks to put down roots and build homes and businesses on land they don't own."

"The newspaper said the railroad can't make any announcements on their lot disposal plan until the Secretary of the Interior tells them what to do," said Jake. "Does he even know what the people up here want?"

"Probably not. That's likely why the newspaper is encouraging all of us here at Ship Creek to tell the government that we want to buy lots, not lease them," said Mac.

"Do you think they know how to listen?" asked Toot.

"Sometimes they do," said Mac. "They originally planned to put this new town about five miles east of here, but after people complained they changed their mind and now they're surveying up here on the site the people wanted."

"So," said Jake, "we all agree that we ought to build our new boarding house in this town, if they decide to sell us a lot?"

"Yep." Mac nodded.

Toot folded his arms tightly across his chest. "Me too, but we need to think about exactly where we want to build our all-board boarding house. Should we be near the bluff or back away from it? Do we want to be on a street or an avenue? Or maybe we want to be on a corner so we'd be on an avenue and a street at the same time."

"You worry too much," said Jake.

In a calm voice Mac said, "Well we do have a little time to think about this. They'll get the streets laid out this week and we can come back up and take a closer look a week from now."

"Good idea, Mac," said Jake. Then, to himself, *Mac always has good ideas.*

The trio breathed easily on the gravity-assisted walk back to the creek bottom. Mac and Toot chatted, but Jake was pensive.

"The survey and clearing crews have been busy as all hell," said Jake. The partners re-climbed the hill the following Sunday and were pleased to see the progress a single week had brought. Contrary to the haphazard tent city arrangement, the new town was laid out on a rectangular grid with lettered streets running north and south and numbered avenues going east and west.

"Not a lot of imagination in this plan," said Toot.

"No, but it's what I'd expect," said Mac, "for a town with restrictions on the kind of business a person can have."

"What kind of restrictions?"

"Moral restrictions," said Mac. "The railroad is authorized the use of public lands along the rail line for town sites and I guess they decided that since they're providing the land they can make the rules. They won't allow bars, gambling parlors or whore houses on any of these lots."

Toot shook his head. "Won't change anyone's morals. Just means those places will be outside of the town."

"Either way, it won't affect our boarding house," said Jake. "We aren't planning to offer sinful living, just clean rooms, clean beds, and good food."

"That'll be a big improvement over those dark smelly cubby holes you're renting in that leaky lopsided tent," said Mac.

"Don't be talking bad about the Bunkhouse Royale," said Toot. "It ain't pretty but it got us started in the business."

"That it did," said Mac as they set off to explore the future streets and avenues of the nameless town. The streets would be wide and the town would flow away from the bluff that fronted the Ship Creek flats.

"The businesses will likely want to be on these streets that run nearest the bluff, like 4th Avenue. Seems like we should put our boarding house a block or so away from the noise and congestion of that commercial area," said Jake.

Toot gazed southward, towards the town's outer limits. "That makes sense to me. Like on 5th Avenue, or maybe clear back along 6th Avenue, where it will always be quiet and peaceful."

"For a boarding house, quiet is good," said Mac. He pointed towards the fringe of the would-be town. "That might be a good area for me to build a house."

Jake waited for an explanation but when there was none he asked, "Can't we all live in the new boarding house? Bachelors don't need their own house."

"Oh I'll be living in our boarding house for now," said Mac. "But I'm thinking of the future. One day I expect I'll want my own house."

"Well if yer thinking of getting hitched you can forget about it," said Toot. "There ain't but a handful of women around here and most of 'em already got husbands."

"There'll be more women here as this town grows," said Mac.

A cross section of the new Alaskans were out enjoying the warm sunny day, sharing picnic lunches with friends as they looked for the perfect lot. Some were dressed in their Sunday best while others were in work clothes. There were a few women, but not many.

"This town doesn't even have a name yet, and that guy who talks in poems is already telling its story," said Toot.

Getting' crowded by the creek, lookin' sad and lookin' bleak.
So Railroad says, "Tear those tents down.
Get away from our crick, and ya better be quick.
Come buy a lot up in our new town.

We've land for sale, far away from our rail.
Big grid 'o roads that all look the same.
Roads with numbers, roads with letters,
But not one road that has a name.

Come catch the action at our big auction,
Pick yer lot and bid 'em high.
We'll build a school and a hospital too,
And a cemetery for them that die.

There'll be a barber and there'll be a banker,
There might even be fine stores.
But there won't be no drinkin' and there won't be no gamblin',
And there certainly won't be no whores."

Inspecting the Government Railroad

H.G. Kaiser, Alaska Railroad Collection; Anchorage Museum,
B1979.002.AEC.G1442

Chapter Thirteen

As the summer solstice slipped quietly by the inevitable march toward winter began anew, but no one at Ship Creek Landing was yet thinking of the cold and dark months far ahead. The now shortening days were still over eighteen hours long and on June 27th the temperature at Fort Yukon, on the top side of the Arctic Circle, was one-hundred degrees.

The railroad community was charged with excitement for the project was gaining momentum on all fronts. Supplies from Seattle and other points were offloaded at the new dock just north of the creek and tracks had been laid from the dock to nearby warehouse facilities and storage yards. About six-hundred workers were employed in the Ship Creek district and four hundred more were working on station man contracts, and the number was growing.

Mac spent his days behind a team of draft horses moving wagon loads of supplies. He went from the dock to designated storage areas and later reloaded the same items and moved them on to supply-eating construction sites. When he returned the team to the railroad barn late one July afternoon his foreman called him aside.

"Lieutenant Mears wants you to come by his office."

Mac visited briefly with Mears whenever their paths crossed but this was different. He was being summoned and in his experience nothing good had ever come from being called to the bosses' office.

"What does Mr. Mears want to see me about?"

"I was just told to have you show up at his office first thing tomorrow."

The evening passed with agonizing slowness as Mac cleaned and re-cleaned his boots and clothes, all the while attempting to divine why Mr. Mears wanted to see him. After a restless night he presented himself at the Commissioner's door first thing in the morning.

"Good morning, Mac."

"Good morning, Mr. Mears."

Mears stood up and extended his hand. "Mac I've come to appreciate your maturity and your serious attitude. I have a job for someone like you. If you're interested, have a seat and we'll talk."

Mac removed his hat and sat in the chair in front of Mears' desk, relieved. "I have no complaints with the job I have now but I'm willing to help out any way that I can."

"What I have in mind will get you a little more pay and might even keep you working through the winter."

Nothing like this had ever happened to Mac. "So what do you need me to do?"

"This project is expanding so fast I can't keep track of everything. There is constant activity right here at Ship Creek and up at the new town site, and now we've started clearing and grading the right-of-way northward. There are engineers supervising the work but they're spread all over Alaska so I rarely see them. The telephone line between here and Seward won't be ready until later this year so I can't even talk to Commissioner Edes."

"It certainly is busy around here," said Mac. "I see more stuff crossing our dock every week."

"And there's more on the way," said Mears. "We're getting six thousand tons of steel rail this summer and some of the equipment from Panama will start arriving before long too."

"From Panama?"

"Yes. We get stuff they no longer need free of charge, except for the shipping expenses. But, free stuff doesn't come without problems. Some of the locomotives were originally purchased by the French back when they bought the Panama Railroad and started digging the Canal, and their rail system used a 5-foot gauge so those locomotives will have to be converted to fit on our standard 4 ft. 8 ½ inch gauge track."

"I expect there will be plenty of problems to solve before this railroad is finished."

"That's why I need someone to help me ride herd on this project, someone who won't be tied to this office dealing with all this damn paperwork." He pointed at the piles of forms, letters and reports covering his large desk. "You would work as my assistant, traveling along the rail corridor taking instructions to the various work sites and bringing their reports back to me. I'd also expect you to keep your eyes open and give me your insights on the progress or problems that you see."

"I'm not an engineer you know."

"You've been with this project from the beginning, you worked for the Tanana Valley Railroad up north before that, and your supervisor and your coworkers speak highly of you. You are the right person for this job."

"Then I'll be happy to work for you, Mr. Mears."

"Good! Like everything around here, we'll have to start with the paperwork. This form will reassign you to me and authorize a pay raise. I've signed it but you need to take it over to Nigel LeCount and have him process it."

"Yes, I've heard of Mr. Nigel."

"When you are finished with him stop by the barn and have that bay mare permanently assigned to you. You'll need good transportation and I'm told you favor that horse."

Mac thought that having the paperwork signed by the Commissioner would make his meeting with Nigel go smoothly, but he was wrong.

"How can I possibly transfer you to a position that does not exist?" asked Nigel.

Mac confidently pointed to the signature on the form, the signature of Nigel's boss, and calmly said, "but this has been approved by Mr. Mears."

"That may well be," said Nigel, holding an oversized document, "but this official Outline of Organization was prepared in Washington, D.C. in accordance with the President's Commission on Economy and Efficiency."

This is one strange fella, thought Mac, *and they say there is an entire city full of folks just like him back east. Makes me damn happy to be up here in Alaska.*

"This Outline of Organization is an exceedingly important tool of administration," said Nigel, still waving the document in Mac's face, "a directive I am duty bound to follow. And, Mr. Mac, there is nothing in this document called a Horse-riding Assistant to the Commissioner."

"Maybe our position description is a bit inaccurate. How about if we leave my title as Laborer and assign me to Mr. Mears?"

"That I can do."

"Can a Laborer have a horse assigned to him?"

"Nothing in the regulations prohibits assigning a horse to a Laborer."

Mac left Nigel's office frustrated by the government, but happy to have his own horse, a new boss and a new, if unofficial, title.

Lot Sale

Pyatt-Laurence Collection; Anchorage Museum,
B1983.146.315

Chapter Fourteen

Residents, businessmen and speculators alike were pleased when the yet nameless town's birthing plan was announced; lots in the new town site would be sold to the highest bidder. July 9th was set as the sale date but the steamer carrying Commissioner Edes to Ship Creek was delayed one day and so was the land sale.

"I'm a bit nervous about the size of this crowd," said Jake to Mac and Toot as they gathered at the town site to finalize their plans.

"Well I'm nervous too," said Toot. "My brain is racing in circles and now my stomach is turning loops too."

Mac shot a serious look at his partners. "Too much worrying weakens the spine. We need to be thinking about buying a lot for our new business. Thirty-two blocks will be available today, from 3rd Avenue to 7th and from B to K Streets. Most blocks have twelve lots so there should be plenty available, even when you consider that they've set some aside for government buildings, schools, wharfs and parks."

"Sounds like they're working real hard to hatch a civilized town," said Jake, "where people can settle down and raise a family."

"You're exactly right," said Mac. "They don't want this to be one of those transient and corrupt 'Hell on Wheels' communities that followed construction of the trans-continental railroad."

Toot, with a serious look now, said, "Ain't bars and whores that worry me. I saw in the paper that a lawyer from Fairbanks is in town and thinking about staying. I'm afraid that if one stays we'll soon have a whole gaggle of them in town."

"What worries me," said Jake, "is that the Commission has already let the contracts to build eleven houses for their permanent employees and now they're talking about putting up a building for bachelor employees to live in. Isn't that going to be competition for this boarding house we're going to build?"

"You boys are getting side tracked by the worries again," said Mac politely. "We'll have plenty of customers if we can find a good cook. But, we won't be needing a cook if we don't get a lot bought today. Did you get a blueprint map of the town site?"

Toot pulled a map from his pocket. "Sure did. Bought one for a dollar from that guy over at the Riverside Hotel."

Mac opened the map and pointed to the lot they'd picked as the perfect site for their new boarding house. "There is a minimum bid of twenty-five dollars. Lots bought for seventy-five dollars or less have to be paid for in cash, but lots selling for more can be purchased with one-third down and five equal annual payments."

Toot watched the crowd congregate in front of the auctioneer's stand. "Now I'm getting nervous again."

"Just keep your shirt on," said Mac, watching huddled groups of men talking softly among themselves. Government rules prohibited bidders from making any arrangements that would restrict bidding or limit competition, but Mac guessed that mostly everyone just wanted to keep their strategies to themselves.

Superintendent of Sales, Andrew Christensen, started the auction promptly at two o'clock, with a speech. "I expect that this new town will become a permanent community in a developing territory. I urge prospective lot owners to relocate from Ship Creek to here as soon as possible."

"Sounds like the Commission is anxious to get the squatters moved away from Ship Creek." Mac whispered to his partners as the sale began. The first property offered was lot one of block forty-four, located on the southwest corner of 4th Avenue and C Street. "This is one of those prime commercial lots," said Mac, "with an appraised value of four hundred dollars.

"Seven hundred dollars," yelled one bidder.

"Seven twenty-five," another countered.

"Seven-fifty."

"Damn overzealous speculators will drive prices right out of our range," said Mac, under his breath.

"Eight hundred and twenty-five dollars, do I hear eight fifty?"

"Eight twenty-five, looking for eight-forty?"

"Eight twenty-five, looking for eight-thirty?"

"Eight hundred and twenty-five dollars, going once, going twice . . . sold to the gentleman in the front row." L. G. Nyberg from Seattle had purchased the first lot in the new town.

Mac watch with interest as sales continued at a brisk pace and commercial lot prices continued to be high. When some lots sold for four times appraised value he too became nervous.

As the afternoon passed the now worry-united partners saw the initial enthusiasm peak, then weaken. Finally, Mac said, "I think they're getting back to our level."

Jake and Toot responded with nervous smiles.

When the auctioneer asked for an opening bid of two hundred dollars on the lot they wanted Mac stretched his already drawn-out body and raised his hand high.

"Two hundred, who'll give me two-fifty?" the auctioneer asked in a voice that was beginning to wear out.

"Two-ten," yelled a bidder from the back of the crowd.

"Two-ten, do I have two-twenty?"

Mac raised his hand.

"Two-thirty," said the voice in the back.

"Will you give me two-forty?" the auctioneer asked, looking directly at Mac.

Mac nodded and Toot sucked air.

"Two-fifty." The anonymous voice again.

Mac motioned yet again when the auctioneer asked for two-sixty.

"Two sixty-five," once more from the rear.

"Two-eighty," Mac yelled out. Toot farted.

When the wearying auctioneer's attempt to get another bid drew only silence the lot was sold to Mac and his partners.

The newly minted tycoons marched to their ground, the place where their dreams would take root. "Now we have to figure out how to get this building put up," said Toot. "I've learned a lot about building and my carpenter buddies will help out when they have time, but we'll have to hire some real help too. And, if we want a real boarding house we're going to have to use real lumber."

Jake pointed toward the dock. "The lumber yard is unloading a freighter right now so there ought to be plenty of boards available."

"What we need is money to buy the lumber with," said Mac. "Not likely they'll give it to us on credit."

"Since the railroad will let us pay for this lot over five years and they aren't charging any interest," said Jake, "why don't we just make the minimum down payment and save our cash to buy lumber. When the boarding house is built we'll have rental income to make the lot payments."

"You're already starting to think like a capitalist," said Mac, "and that's good. There were about 600 lots sold today so this town is going to take off fast and we're going to have to work hard to keep up."

White House Hotel

P.S. Hunt, Alaska Railroad Collection; Anchorage Museum, B1979.002.AEC.G541

Chapter Fifteen

The still unnamed town changed rapidly after the first lot sale. Clearing and construction began almost overnight and H Street from the beach to the town site was soon cleared and readied for use. Within two weeks commercial and residential buildings began to spring up, and work was soon underway on a post office.

"Most folks are calling the new town Anchorage," said Mac to Lieutenant Mears.

"I know, but now the Governor wants to name the town Matanuska."

"There is certainly no shortage of ideas. I've heard some want to name the town Alaska City."

"Someone even proposed 'Terminal' as the name."

"Seems like the people living here ought to decide," said Mac.

"We each get a hundred and fifty bucks, which works out to about sixty cents an hour, and that's more than we'd get as railroad employees," Jake said to the Damn Yankees. He'd turned in the properly approved paperwork on their first contract and collected their pay. "Let's celebrate with a hot breakfast," he said as he and the men sat at the counter of the Montana Cafe, the first business in the new town.

"What'll it be men?" asked the all-in-one manager, server and dishwasher.

"Flapjacks and coffee," said Jake.

"Black pudding," said Paddy

"Smorgas,"

"bougatsa,"

"kasha,"

"wurst," the others said in turn.

"Flapjacks and coffee for six," the man yelled at the cook.

"You sure they ordered flapjacks?" asked Jake.

"Don't matter, that's all the cook knows how to make."

"So why'd you ask what we want?"

"Best customer service in town is the motto in this establishment."

"But so far you are the only restaurant in town."

"And we have the best customer service!"

The eatery's hectic morning rush passed quickly as workers pushed down flapjacks and hot coffee and headed off to construction jobs. The Damn Yankees loitered, drank more coffee, and listened in as the conversation among the remaining customers turned to the town name.

"Matanuska, babushka, all sounds Russian to me," said one. "And, even though we bought this land from Russia it really wasn't theirs to sell, and the folks who'd been living here for thousands of years weren't even considered."

"I don't think Alaska City is the right name either," said another, looking out the window. "We're in Alaska alright, but I don't think we're a city yet, with mud streets and all."

"Terminal would have been a good name for my marriage," said yet another, "from the honeymoon on. I'm hoping this town will last a bit longer."

Jake interrupted the discussion, getting the Damn Yankees attention. "Plumb-bob has offered us another contract. Are we ready to go back to work?"

"Aye, yah sure, ne, da, ja!"

The railroad's designated town site manager announced plans to build a city wharf and a water system, and the feverish pace in town was matched by the pace on the railroad project. Buildings were going up along Ship Creek and track was being laid in the rail yard. Locomotives and rail cars and steam shovels arrived from

Panama. The Damn Yankees and other station man crews leap frogged their way northward, clearing and grading, and track gangs followed close behind. The twin steel rails marched steadily into the Alaskan wilderness.

With help from his carpenter friends Toot sketched plans for the new boarding house. The two-story building would have a front parlor on the main floor where the residents could spend their leisure time, with a kitchen and dining area at the rear. On the second level were small private sleeping rooms and two large communal sleeping rooms. A small bathroom at the end of the upstairs hallway served all residents.

"How soon can we get this built?" asked Mac as he reviewed the drawings with his business partners.

"Depends on how much time we have to work on it," said Toot. "You and I can do much of the work and Jake will help when he's in town. Some of my carpenter buddies will help out when they can. With hard work we should be able to have it closed in before the first snowfall."

"We can do that if we set our minds to it," said Mac.

Toot shook his partners hand. "Before winter gets here we're gonna have the best damn boarding house in Anchorage, or Matanuska or Terminal or Alaska City."

"If we keep the boards straight, square, plumb and level everything will fit together nicely," said Toot.

By day he and the railroad carpenter crews were busy constructing homes for the permanent Commission employees with families in Alaska. Each evening the skills he gained by working alongside the journeyman carpenters, along with pockets full of nails, accompanied him to the bunkhouse project.

The partners worked with entrepreneurial enthusiasm throughout the summer, juggling their day jobs with evening and week-end bunkhouse building.

"You have learned carpentering." Mac complimented Toot as they admired their just built walls late one evening."

There was a crispness in the air on the September week-end when they nailed the final shingles on the roof. Toot set his hammer aside. "Soon as we get the windows in this place will be weather-tight."

Mac looked up at the beautiful yet prophetic dusting of snow on the Chugach. "We best be getting that done real soon then."

"We've made good progress this summer," said Mears. He and Mac strode across the creek bottom on a sunny fall day. The area was beginning to look like a rail yard as residents moved up to the new town site and the temporary tent city was replaced by more permanent railroad facilities.

"More than I figured we'd get done. I wasn't sure how this disjointed approach would function, with some workers on a contract and others on the payroll."

"Different solutions to different challenges," said Mears. "Right now both methods are getting results. The high iron is moving north."

"The line between here and Seward should take shape quickly," said Mac, "Now that we own the old Alaska Northern line."

"We still have plenty to do down there," said Mears. "The existing line still needs refurbishment, and of course the line was never built beyond Kern Creek a few miles south of Girdwood."

"At least the name-the-town debate is finally over."

"Yeah," said Mears. "Looks like we'll be living in Anchorage, Alaska."

Anchorage, First Snow, October 8, 1915

Marie Silverman Collection; Anchorage Museum,
B1963.016.6

Chapter Sixteen

Winter's arrival was heralded first by cold and darkness and then by snow. The cold and darkness crept up in measured steps but the snow arrived with alacrity and covered Anchorage with the first layer of a white blanket that would mushroom in the coming months.

Outdoor construction season ended abruptly but with their building roofed, windowed and heated the bunkhouse partners had won the race against the change of seasons.

"This place is gonna be warm and cozy," said Toot. They stood around the large pot-bellied stove that was the centerpiece of the front parlor. The ornate stove's square four-legged base and door were polished metal, as were the decorative rim and regal crown above. The stove, with help from the big cook stove in the rear kitchen, provided heat for the entire building. Ceiling vents channeled the leftover heat to the second floor where the lukewarm air facilitated sleeping and promoted bathroom expediency. The interior walls were framed but the wooden lath that would provide the base for the plaster walls had not yet arrived.

"The lumber yard said they ordered 'em," Toot explained to his partners, "but they ain't arove yet."

"These walls won't get finished until next spring," said Mac. "Even if the lath does get here we still don't have enough horsehair." The long hair that Mac was collecting from the tails and manes of the horses at the railroad barn would strengthen the plaster.

"So what'll we do for privacy until then?" asked Jake.

"We'll do without," said Toot. "Won't hurt nuthin."

"Well it might hurt business," said Jake. "People aren't likely to rent rooms that have see-through walls."

"In this town they will," said Mac. "We may have to offer a discount until we get the walls plastered, but this cold weather will make folks damn happy to get out of those drafty canvas tents they're living in now."

"Then we best get our sign hung out and gather up some customers," said Jake.

Mac looked at his partners. "We don't have a sign."

"We've still got the Bunkhouse Royale sign," said Toot. "Nothing wrong with it!"

"Guess it'll have to do."

"Sure will," said Toot. When he hung the old but freshly altered NEW Bunkhouse Royale sign above the front door the almost finished boardinghouse was open for business.

Jake's station man partners became the first bunkhouse tenants. With the no-walls discount the rate was affordable and included two hot meals each day. "Ve make you da bargain," Sven said to Mac one evening soon after he and his friends had moved in. "Ve can hunt and fish to get da meat for dat fat cook to burn up. Dat save you da money."

"Aye, ne, da, ja!"

"We can work out a deal," said Mac. "Using wild game instead of high-priced Anchorage groceries will keep us well fed and give you boys something to do besides hang around at Poetic Pete's pool hall all winter."

The railroad's new recreation facility provided entertainment for railroad workers; magazines, a billiards table and even a phonograph. And, Poetic Pete entertained the men with his latest verse.

My full-time work comes with a perk;
The new pool hall is my office.
But I'm a nincompoop and my job is duck soup,
So most folks say I'm worthless.

All day long I hum a happy song,
As I sit and watch them records spin.
To pass the time I make words rhyme,
With toes a tappin' and a giant grin.

I don't do much but blather and such,
But of being fired I have no fear.
For while some call me an idiot, others say I'm brilliant,
And the difference ain't always clear.

With no work to be done, my job's to have fun.
'Tis a bit of a sham, I cannot deny.
I'm one of them nitwits with a title that fits,
I am the Railroad's CFI.

Mac, anticipating being laid off for the season, was pleased when Mears said, "I need you to stay on for the winter. We must get everything in place so we'll be ready to restart construction work first thing next spring, and I need your help."

"You know I'll be happy to have the work," said Mac, "and I know we expect to make big strides next year."

"We do, but we got a decent start this year," said Mears. He leaned back in his chair and began counting on his fingers:

Thumb, "We cleared forty miles of right-of-way to the north of here, thirty-four of those miles have been graded and fourteen miles of track have been laid;"

Index finger, "We laid side track at the Anchorage terminal and erected several buildings;"

Middle finger, "We sold nearly nine hundred lots in Anchorage for private businesses and homes, built fifteen modern homes for married Commission personnel and quarters for single employees;"

Ring finger, "We built a log hospital to meet the President's directive to provide for the health of those building the railroad."

"Don't forget the reconstruction work in Seward," said Mac. "The track renovations allow freight and passenger service between Seward and mile thirty-four via a gas powered rail car."

"That's true," said Mears, grabbing his pinky, the last unused finger. "And though construction hasn't started on the north end, the survey work has been completed between Broad Pass and Fairbanks. Next year we'll be working all along the line."

As the year drew to a close there were already one hundred and fifty students in the Anchorage school and about fifteen hundred residents in the town. That number grew by one on December 25, 1915 when Jane Wainwright Mears gave birth to their third child, Frederick Mears III, in the log hospital. The war in Europe was beginning to weigh on people's minds, but most were focused on the spring of 1916 when full-scale construction would begin on the government railroad in Alaska.

PART THREE
The Rail Line Emerges
(1916 - 1917)

Freight Team on Winter Trail

Frederick C. Mears Papers,
UAF-1984-75-17, Archives, University of Alaska Fairbanks

Chapter Seventeen

"FIRE!" The single word that instantly grips then stirs the soul, echoed through the Seward rail terminal on January 22, 1916. The wharf was ablaze and despite the heroic efforts of railroad employees and townspeople alike the conflagration quickly consumed the wooden structure.

"I suppose the good news is that no one was hurt and they were able to confine the damage to the wharf area," was all Mears said to Mac when the news reached Anchorage. Mac saw that Mears' rigid facial muscles suggested an inner tension, but knew that in engineer fashion he would catalog the lesson and remain focused on the work ahead.

It was the depth of the Alaskan winter, dark and cold, tedious and taxing, and construction activity was at a standstill but preparation for the next season was already under way.

"I need you to ride up north today," said Mears. "Building the branch line out to the coal fields is a top priority for this season and we need to be absolutely certain the construction materials are in place before the snow melts. I'd like you to make a personal inspection and assure that everything is on schedule."

"I know a horse that will appreciate the exercise," said Mac, slowly untangling his tall frame from the unadorned office chair and donning his heavy coat and the wolf-skin cap that replaced his cowboy hat during the winter months. When properly dressed, he knew, the arctic winter was an entirely enjoyable experience.

At the railroad barn Lucky greeted him with unconditional devotion and with Mac astride set out with the eagerness that comes from being too long in the stable, breath steaming smoke-like into the biting dry air. Frost formed on her long face as she settled into a sustainable pace. The heat from the big animal's body comforted Mac as they rode northward along the well-used winter trail. As the late morning sun peeked above the horizon the clear sky begetting the bitter cold turned a deep blue. Thick hoarfrost dressed the spruce trees in matching sequined gowns and the muffled footsteps were quickly absorbed by winter's crushing silence.

Mac affectionately patted the horse's neck as they moved as one through the woods, blending into the surreal combination of cold silence and stark beauty. Mac typically found this uniquely Alaskan experience invigorating but today, blindsided by thoughts of his first love, he was as lonely as the winter forest. *His life had taken purpose,* he recalled, *when as a teen he'd courted the preacher's daughter. On blissful Sunday afternoons they'd strolled hand-in-hand, watching the children play and sharing unspoken dreams of a life together. When she died his life reversed, and attempts to mend his broken heart with alcohol launched the wild boom-and-bust existence that now defined his life.*

The cornerstone of his current scheme to break the self-destructive cycle was an Anchorage home site, purchased when they became available for the twenty-five-dollar minimum bid. In the solitude of his mind he built the house he would one day share with a fine wife, but reality contradicted his dreams for there were few prospective brides in a land populated largely by men.

Mac's melancholy thoughts were interrupted by the sound of an approaching team pulling a sled along the winter trail, delivering spikes, tie plates and other hardware from the end-of-rail to designated staging areas along the rail route to the north. "Whoa, hold up there," the teamster instructed the big horses as he pulled gently on the lines. "You picked a chilly day for a ride," he said as Mac and the mare stopped alongside.

Mac wiped his nose with his sleeve. "The air is a bit sharp this morning, but the man I work for thinks it's a good day for me to inventory the stuff you fellas are hauling."

"There are stockpiles all along here," the driver said, pointing a heavily mittened hand up the trail.

"Sounds like you're off to a great start," Mac said to the driver. "Think you'll have it wrapped up before spring?"

"Nothing to fret about; we'll get the job done. We have good teams, great drivers and you know this snow trail won't be melting any time soon."

"Winter is sometimes our best friend," said Mac. "This packed snow makes a fine sled route."

The teamster rubbed his hands together. "And frozen rivers and streams are easy to cross." Then, with a nearly imperceptible flick of the lines, "Gid up now."

The railroad building process was becoming clear in Mac's head. *Clear the right-of-way and then grade the roadbed, put down a layer of stone ballast, install about three thousand wooden cross ties, add tie plates, spike lengths of steel rail fast and bolt them together; then do the same thing for each of the four hundred and seventy-three miles that will make up the railroad. Difficulties arise when the routine becomes inadequate: where the ground is unstable, where the line abuts big rivers and where rivers and streams are crossed. Plumb-bob and the other engineers will manage the routine and overcome the adversities with a unique solution for each unique problem. Beyond the engineering challenges are the managerial challenges Commissioner Mears faces each day: securing funding in a timely manner, juggling the conflicting demands of politicians, community leaders and labor leaders, coordinating the work of disparate managers working in disjointed locations and, above all, providing for the safety and welfare of all workers.* Mac's job description did not require that he share the Commissioner's burdens, but his character did.

Today's task was a straightforward exercise; count the items at each site, compare the count to the report and note any discrepancies. Except, this was being conducted in the heart of Alaska exactly when winter, his sometimes friend, had turned the stockpiles to steel-cored icebergs. The snow and deep-frozen steel hardware required heavy mittens, yet the requisite pencil work was impossible with covered hands and Mac's bare fingers soon stiffened with cold.

By the time the job was complete he was exhausted and near frozen but his spirits were high for he knew he could inform Mr. Mears that the inventory reports were reliable and the stockpiling effort was on schedule.

Daylight had faded long before Mac returned his horse to the railroad barn and trudged up the hill to Anchorage, the deep frozen snow creaking underfoot. In the bunkhouse parlor tenants were feeding coal through the hinged door of the ornate yet functional stove. In the surrounding warmth problems were resolved, plans were made, dreams were shared, and the latest railroad gossip was passed on.

"Either the kitchen is on fire or supper is about ready," one of the residents said as Mac walked in. "How many ways can that cook think of to ruin good moose meat?"

The others looked at the smoke drifting from the combination kitchen and dining room and laughed, but not loudly enough for the cook to hear them.

The men shuffled aside to clear a stove-side spot for the frosty version of Mac. His now close association with Commissioner Mears made him a reliable source of railroad news, so he had only a moment to thaw before one asked, "Any rumors from headquarters?"

"There are," said Mac, staying close to the hot stove. "Sounds like the railroad plans to change its mind and run the main line right through Anchorage."

"I thought the plan was to run the high iron east of town along the Chugach foothills," said the man, "and make the five miles of rail between the foothills and Ship Creek a spur to the rail yards."

Mac turned to warm his other side. "It was, but now they decided to route the main line into Anchorage from the south, cross over the mouth of the marsh and swing along the shore of the inlet to Ship Creek. Guess they decided Anchorage is going to be too important to bypass."

The conversation ended abruptly when the fat cook yelled, "come and get it," and the men scrambled for places at the communal table, actions disputing words.

Early Winter in Anchorage

P.S. Hunt, Dr. Romig Photograph Collection; Anchorage Museum,
Loan from the Anchorage School District, B1977.005.4

Chapter Eighteen

"Flapjacks, special of the day," said the cook as he slammed the steaming stack of sourdough cakes on the table in front of Mac. Winter breakfast at the NEW Bunkhouse Royale was a two stage affair, with an early feeding for the working men followed by a more leisurely repast for the seasonally unemployed. When Mac continued to stare into his coffee mug, ignoring the hot jacks, the cook asked, "And what might we be stewing about this damned early in the morning?"

"Labor problems have been worrying the Commissioner and now I've got a case of the worries too."

"What the hell are you talking about? Most railroaders are happy with their work."

"I thought so too, and no one cares more about these workers than Mr. Mears, but some folks are trying to get a union organized, claiming that the railroad is violating some law limiting the number of hours a federal employee can work each day."

"I don't get what the damn problem is," said the cook. "Those workers want the extra hours and the extra pay."

Mac planted his elbows on the table and rested his chin on his clasped fist, a concerned look in his eyes. "That has me befuddled too."

"Well you best eat some breakfast. You have a busy day ahead of you."

With Mac and the others out the door the Damn Yankees gathered around the big kitchen table for more flapjacks, followed by mug upon mug of hot coffee.

"Close the damn door," the cook yelled as Jake pushed his way into the kitchen lugging a full coal scuttle. "It's colder than all hell out there."

"Still thirty below—," said Jake.

"Brrrrrrr," the men responded as one.

Jake continued, "Or colder. That thermometer only registers to minus thirty, and all the mercury has been hiding down in the bulb for several days now. We need to find a thermometer that's made for Alaska."

"Or Nor-duh-KHO-ta," said Sven.

Jake set the coal aside while removing his heavy coat, hat and mittens, then turned to Sven. "You helped build the Great Northern Railway across the top of North Dakota and Montana, so I'm sure you can teach us some lessons about living and working in relentless cold. Like having a thermometer that registers to fifty below zero."

"Yah, and—"

"Warm clothing and boots."

"Yah."

"And good tools, with wooden handles."

"Yah."

"And hearty workers, like you Swedes."

"Yah sure."

"At least it's warm in here," said Jake. He moved the coal closer to the cook stove, being careful not to touch the long johns drying on the makeshift clothes line strung near the heat source. "This ought to keep the coal eating son-of-a-bitch happy for an hour or two."

"We wouldn't use so damn much coal if we weren't trying to heat all of Alaska," the cook said. "Most of our heat goes out through these drafty damn walls."

"That'll get better when we get the walls plastered."

"Let's hope that coal pile out back lasts until then," the cook said, before turning his attention to the stack of dirty dishes on the kitchen counter. "Who's washing dishes today? And don't look at me like you don't understand." He looked around the table and was met only by silent stares. "Tell you what, I'll teach you boys to play poker and then we can play a friendly card game to decide who's going to wash the dishes."

"Yah sure, you betcha," said Sven immediately, his voice working again.

"The game is called five card draw," the cook said, then explained the hierarchy of winning card combinations.

The men sat quietly, listening intently, Jake observed. He knew that in a game where those who say the least win the most the Damn Yankees would be naturals. They understood the numbers and soon recognized a winning hand even if they weren't sure what it was called.

Each week they added new facets to the game and soon equal piles of match sticks were handed out as faux betting became part of the morning routine.

Through the winter months the sub-zero cold poured down from the arctic and hung over Cook Inlet until low pressure from the north pacific pushed the frigid air away and brought snow. Then the cycle would repeat. As the cold days and weeks passed the Damn Yankees perfected their poker game and railroad supplies kept moving. By late March the days again matched the nights in length and the bunkhouse thermometer was back in the working range.

"Any one go on strike today?" one of the men asked Mac as they relaxed in the parlor digesting a busy day and their evening meal.

"All is quiet for the moment," said Mac, "but I'm afraid there is more to come. There have only been small strikes so far, but I don't think this new Alaska Federal Labor Union is finished yet. And, Mr. Mears is convinced that his actions are consistent with those of other railroads and in compliance with government rules."

Following their cold weather drill the bunkhouse men loafed by the warm stove throughout the evening and then one by one dashed off to their warm beds in the cold rooms with imaginary walls. Mac went to bed with the myriad of reports that flowed into the Commissioner's office dancing through his head. *Financial reports with dollars spent versus dollars budgeted. Staffing reports telling how many people worked, where, doing what. Inventory reports listing items needed, on hand and in transit. Progress reports detailing acres cleared, cubic yards of material moved, miles of right-of-way cleared, and miles of right-of-way graded.*

When the data on these numbers reports, as Mac called them, showed problems developing it was Mr. Mears' job to resolve them. With the problems under control the combined force of the little numbers would expand the big number, miles of railway completed. Only when the big number reached four-seventy-three would the railroad through Alaska be complete.

Rubberneck Car

Alaska State Library, Clarence L. Andrews Photograph Collection,
Clarence Andrews, ASL-P45-0564

Chapter Nineteen

"This union issue is like a keg of dynamite," said Mac to Toot as they ambled along the tidal zone of the again ice-free inlet on a late April evening.

Toots' breath vaporized in the still cool air as he examined one of the large muddy ice blocks littering the shore. "Everything is under control now, ain't it?"

"For the moment, but things were tense as hell the past few weeks."

Toot looked surprised. "That's puttin' it a tad bit kind. The tension was so damn thick you could see it in the air. Reckon that's why Mears asked the government to send in troops."

"But instead Washington sent a conciliation committee."

Toot shook his head. "And I still don't understand why the union called a strike before the committee even got their work done."

"Didn't make sense to me either," said Mac, "but the tension went sky high when they finally sent troops from Valdez to protect the men Mears was hiring to replace the striking workers."

"That was a difficult time," said Toot, "especially for those of us who weren't part of the strike. I know we were all happy as hell when the committee raised the base wages and the whole thing was resolved."

Mac gazed across the inlet, looking to the southwest. "You know Mt. Augustine is less than two hundred miles away from here, dormant now but still plenty explosive. Just like this union issue."

With building materials again available Toot and Jake started plastering and painting the bunkhouse walls, and the source of the no-walls discount rapidly disappeared. Sven watched with a worried look on his typically jovial face.

"Yah sure, dat bargain vas too goot for lasting."

By the time Mac helped his partners hang the doors that finally enclosed the rooms Sven and the other Damn Yankees were as noisy and incomprehensible as a coop full of clucks, but fell silent when the owners sat down to discuss the future of the now walled NEW Bunkhouse Royale.

"This place turned out better than I expected it would," said Jake, looking at the freshly painted private rooms.

"What the hell did you expect?" asked Toot.

"Oh I always knew we could build a decent place, but this is better than decent."

"That's why we don't have empty beds," said Mac.

"And when we're full up," said Jake, "we take in enough money to make our debt payments, buy supplies and pay the cook. And we still have a little money left over."

The men had divided the bunkhouse management duties according to their skills and availability. Mac remained an active manager even though his rapidly expanding railroad responsibilities sometimes limited his availability. Toot took care of construction and maintenance and Jake, a natural with the figures, handled the finances. Unnaturally for him, he also became their representative in the Anchorage business community and Chamber of Commerce.

Mac glanced at his business partners, then turned to the breathless group of worried faces standing nearby, looking at him as though their silence made them invisible. "Then there is no reason to raise the rates."

"Yah sure," said Sven with a giant grin that was soon replicated by his friends.

"Aye, ne, da, ja!"

As the tongue waggling began anew Mac interrupted with a stern, "But, we're running an honest business here."

"Well we're mostly honest," said Toot. "Some of this wild game the boys are providing might not be exactly legal, but that's kind of a gray area."

"It's the gambling that'll get us in trouble," said Mac. "We have a successful business going, let's not ruin it by getting crosswise with the government."

"No gambling going on here," said Jake. "But there are big poker games in the back rooms of some places almost every night. And there is booze in town too."

"Just don't let your crew get caught up in anything illegal," said Mac.

Mac knew the Commission would tackle the town's illicit drinking and gambling activities in good time. But, the tone of today's meeting with Mears and Nigel reminded him that the first order of business was building a railroad. For that they needed money, which came to them by way of the government's system. Except, Mac thought, *the word system can't be applied to the federal funding scheme unless it is preceded by "cockamamie" or "harebrained". The federal fiscal year begins and ends in midsummer, the peak of the short Alaskan construction cycle, and orders for summer supplies have to be submitted to the Commission's Purchasing Agent in Seattle the prior January. All this before politics and bureaucracy are stirred in. Truly a counterproductive approach to an Alaskan construction project.*

"Congress wants this railroad built," said Commissioner Mears to Mac and Nigel, "but they won't give us the money to pay our bills. We were nearly out of money last fall."

Nigel rolled his eyes. "They appropriated two million dollars to allow us to continue work until the 1st of July."

"Yeah, at the end of February, and that almost didn't get approved," said Mears, "thanks to that perpetual pain-in-the-ass in Seward. He circulated those contrived stories demeaning the railroad, and he was the one who stirred up the opposition when our two-million-dollar appropriation was before the House Committee on Territories." Mears looked squarely at Nigel now. "I wish I knew where that scoundrel gets all of his information?"

Nigel ignored the question but appeared to listen closely as Mears reiterated the importance of getting new funding in place before July.

"I understand sir," said the accountant as he packed his brief-case and prepared to leave.

As Nigel departed Mac gazed through the window of Mr. Mears' office, seeing a perfectly framed view of new buildings and rail cars moving on a spider's web of track crisscrossing the rail yard. "Starting to look like a railroad here."

"Not only here. The new dock is being built in Seward, and the workers that just arrived at Nenana are already busy building a dock on the south bank of the Tanana River. But I can't get out to check on these things because I'm busy running a tourist camp," said Mears, waving a sheet of paper in front of Mac. "They think I have nothing better to do than give guided tours to visiting dignitaries."

Mac maintained a serious look and simply said, "Yes sir." He'd observed the increasing number of well-dressed curiosity seekers, had even been drafted to help with the tour guide duties from time to time.

Mears no-nonsense tone remained. "I understand why they want to tour Alaska in the summer, but I don't have time to be their babysitter. I'm going to have to build a damn Rubberneck Car just to haul them all around in."

"A Rubberneck Car, sir?"

"Yeah, we had one in Panama to haul official visitors up and down the railroad. Take this photograph over to the wrench bend-ers and tell them to build one just like this."

Mac looked at the picture as he walked across to the large me-chanical shop. The rolling tourist platform was a flat car topped with several rows of front-facing seats, elevated theater-like from front to rear. The car was open-sided to maximize viewing oppor-tunities and covered with a convex roof.

"What in the hell is that?" the Chief Mechanic yelled as he looked at the small photo. "That's the strangest damn looking rail-car I've ever seen."

"He called it a Rubberneck Car," Mac said, accustomed to the mechanic's volatility and indelicate language.

"I thought I'd seen every sonofabitchin' kind of rail car there was, but this is a new one on me. But we can sure as hell build the ugly ass thing."

"Mr. Mears will appreciate that."

"Why is it so important to have the shitass seats elevated?" the mechanic asked.

"That way," Mac said, "each special visitor will think they have the best seat in the house."

"We should have almost one hundred and fifty miles of line in operation by freeze-up," said Mears to Mac as they reviewed the July numbers reports.

The big number, thought Mac as he silently did the calculating. "At this rate we'll have this line finished in two or three more years."

"It isn't that simple I'm afraid. The miles we are picking up from the Alaska Northern line are refurbishment. The new construction will take longer and some areas are going to be very slow going, like along Turnagain Arm. There are a lot of bridges to build too, especially up in the Talkeetna area."

"And then there are the big bridges," said Mac, "Like Hurricane Gulch and the Tanana River."

"Those and more."

"So I don't have to start looking for a new job just yet?"

"Not for a long time Mac."

That August, on the down side of summer, Mears informed Mac that Commissioner Edes was finally in Alaska, along with his wife. "He's inspecting the work in Seward now but he'll be up here soon and I'll need you to help me play tour guide for a few days."

When the Edes entourage appeared Mac was part of the reception party. "We appreciate you taking the time to show us around," said Commissioner Edes as he was introduced to Mears' horse-riding assistant and sometimes tour guide. "I know things are busy up here."

"Always busy here," said Mac.

While touring the Matanuska branch line and other construction activity in the area above Knik Arm Edes explained the challenges he'd faced getting the railroad's funding through Congress earlier in the year. "Representative Curry from California is solidly behind us, but Representative Cannon from Illinois opposes us, so I have to fight like hell for every nickel we get."

"And I hear that Mr. Cannon is the sometimes mouth piece of Mr. Ballaine in Seward."

"The two are very close," said Edes, "and I'm afraid their motives and methods aren't always honorable. Unfortunately, that is something I see a lot of in Washington."

Alaska's fireweed display their distinctive purple blossoms bottom to top as the season progresses so when Mac noticed that the tattle-tale plants had topped out he knew the summer would soon be over, and Mr. Edes would soon be heading south.

Before leaving Alaska Edes got a firsthand look at the challenges to be faced in building the rail line along the bank of the Susitna River, and across the unstable walls of the Nenana River canyon. "I'll be sure Secretary Lane is aware of the construction challenges being faced in Alaska, and assure him that most politically influential Alaskan's are strong supporters of the project," said Edes to Mears and Mac as he departed for Washington, D.C.

Washout Near Peter's Creek

P.S. Hunt, Alaska Railroad Collection; Anchorage Museum,
B1979.002.AEC.G147

Chapter Twenty

Mac was pleased with the Anchorage he saw in the fall of 1916. The booming town's forty-five hundred residents already enjoyed many modern conveniences and now, just in time for winter, electric lights were being installed in the bunkhouse. Yet, in the town spawned by the railroad and fueled by railroad money he saw a love-hate relationship developing between offspring and parent. There was friction between Commissioner Mears and the local Chamber of Commerce over utilization of dock facilities. Some residents were angry about the Commission's ban on gambling and liquor, some were jealous of the comfortable houses being built for railroad officials, and some of the bunkhouse residents even resented the congestion that the rapid growth had created in their town.

"Thought I'd never get home," a frustrated boarder complained as he returned to the NEW Bunkhouse Royale late one afternoon. "I'm trying to get across 4th Avenue and there was an automobile coming at me from the east, so I stand there and wait. When the noisy thingamajig passes another one is coming from the west, so there I stand waiting again! We should put a limit on the number of those contraptions that are allowed in this town."

"We sure as shootin' should," said the fat cook. "Last I heard there are already twenty-five automobiles here in Anchorage and that by damn is enough!"

"Don't worry," said Mac. "Winter will soon be here and it'll be too cold to get the damn things started."

"Don't be saying that word yet," said Toot. "We're trying like hell to get all these new buildings enclosed so we can do the interior work through the winter, but we ain't near ready for freeze-up."

As the heavy autumn rains falling on the mountains and foothills north of Anchorage rushed toward Cook Inlet they found the previously unrestricted drainage near Peter's Creek blocked by the new rail line. Unable to squeeze through the inadequate drainage the muddy flow swirled behind the embankment until the water overflowed the track. The again uncontained force destroyed the rail bed as it rushed through, leaving the rail unsupported and unpassable.

"We've work to do today," said Mac to Lucky as they headed out in the early morning to assess the damage. The sun had taken the chill off the day by the time Mac arrived at the washout but his mood remained frosty.

"We'll have the line reopened in a couple days," the maintenance foreman said as he scurried over to greet Mac. "We have a car load of piling on the way, and a pile driver." As they examined the gaping void beneath the dangling rail line the foreman said, "If the damn construction people had built this right in the first place the track wouldn't have washed out."

"That's interesting," said Mac, "because the construction foreman told me this morning that the washout was most likely caused by poor maintenance. And I expect if a train happens along and runs off the broken track you'll both blame the train crew!"

The foreman puffed up and his face reddened, but he was smart enough to keep whatever words were boiling up in his brain from getting out. Mac gave him a moment, then said, "What we need to do right now is get this track fixed and get this rail line back open."

On the ride back to town Mac pondered his latest lesson in Alaskan railroading. *This rail line is a just a fragile thread connecting distant points, but Alaska prefers to remain unthreaded and will fight back every chance she gets. Keeping this line open will always be a challenge, but real solutions won't be found until these railroaders start looking for answers instead of scapegoats. If they don't, this gravy train we are all riding on could go under just like the other rail lines up here have.*

Mac and his partners were relieved to find the NEW Bunkhouse Royale filled to capacity as the Damn Yankees and others who'd spent their summer in construction camps moved back in just as others left to go south for the winter. Coal was now being delivered into Anchorage by railroad from a small mine near the Matanuska Branch at Moose Creek and the big parlor stove was once more aglow.

"The boys want to give you cooking lessons," Jake said to the fat cook as the Damn Yankees looked on. "They've been eating camp-fire cooked moose, salmon and boiled oats all summer long so I reckon they're anxious for some fancier fare."

The cook met the stares of the Damn Yankees. "I taught you to play poker so now you're going to show me how to fix the grub you ate back in Transylvania or Pennsylvania or wherever in hell it is you all come from?"

"Aye, yah sure, ne, da, ja!"

Creativity was the hallmark of the international cooking classes and there were few boundaries. As he served the evening's mystery meal one cold winter evening the cook asked a guest, "Do you know how to tell the difference between moose meat and bear meat?"

"No."

"I didn't think so," the fat cook roared, laughing along with his new teachers. "Neither could Poetic Pete."

One of the winter ploys of the Bunkhouse boys,
To stave off the winter blues,
Was to hang around the kitchen fillin' that cauldron,
With the stuff of their favorite stews.

They invited me to share their special evening fare,
Though of their menu they gave no hints.
And they'd never reveal the fixin's of that meal,
But I ain't seen my sled dog since.

When Mac sat down with Commissioner Mears in his office at the new General Office Building, the Gee-Oh-Bee everyone called it, to help prepare the Commission's annual report for 1916, he knew his boss was pleased with the progress they could report.

"There are over one hundred and forty miles of railroad in operation," said Mears as he looked over the reports. "An additional one hundred and seventy-five miles of right-of-way are cleared and fifty-seven of those are graded."

And, Mac knew, when Emma Duke drove the first spike on the Fairbanks Division back in October the high iron began moving southward from Interior Alaska, reaching for the line snaking northward from Seward and Cook Inlet.

"There is good reason to be proud of the progress we've made this year," said Mears, "but I'm very concerned about the rising cost. Shipping capacity has been limited by the war, and that's driven freight rates up so the price of steel rail, tie plates and spikes has increased dramatically. The mile of railroad that cost $9,860 to build last year cost us $11,082 to build this year."

"But you're still expecting to have trains operating from Seward to Fairbanks by 1921 or maybe even 1920 aren't you?" asked Mac.

"I am. But I'm also an Army Captain now, and very concerned about the escalating war in Europe. I've read the grim accounts of Verdun and the Somme where hundreds of thousands died along stagnant battle lines, and even though Woodrow Wilson was re-elected I expect the United States will ultimately become entangled in that European tragedy."

New Alaska Engineering Commission Hospital

Frank W. Mondell's AEC Photo Album,
UAF-2013-159-17, Archives, University of Alaska Fairbanks

Chapter Twenty-one

The teapot sizzling on the parlor stove belied the bitter cold lurking just outside the NEW Bunkhouse Royale. Thick frost coated the window panes and the relentless arctic air crept soundlessly under the door and through the thin clapboard walls. The outside temperature climbed to ten degrees below zero during the heat of the day but each night the mercury again retreated into the bulb.

January is a trying month in Anchorage, thought Mac. *December offers holiday festivities and February brings notably longer days, but January features only the endless cold and darkness that slowly but surely erode the spirit of even us seasoned Alaskans. And now war worries have been added to the assemblage of winter ghosts haunting vulnerable minds.*

Mac, Toot and the others fortunate enough to have winter jobs bundled up and left the bunkhouse early each morning. When they returned in the evening their cheeks were aglow, their beards were frosted and clear viscous fluid dripped from their noses, but their minds were ghost free. To stave off cabin fever the other residents ventured out whenever possible during the short day, some to visit Anchorage cafes and businesses, some to hang out at the recreation center at the railroad terminal where Poetic Pete did his best to entertain off-duty and out-of-work railroad workers. There they visited with other idle workers, played matchstick poker and read the latest issues of newspapers and magazines. Favorite magazines were often tucked inside coats and brought back to the bunkhouse parlor to be read and reread until the pages wore thin.

"Braunschweiger," said Hans as he and the cook put the finishing touches on the evening's main fare. The Damn Yankees continued to fill their idle winter hours by introducing the fat cook to their favorite old country dishes. The assembled men looked curiously at the stove, gave it a quick nose test and continued their pre-dinner conversation.

"Rumor is the railroad has big plans for this summer," one of the men said, looking at Mac.

"We're anxious to get the rail line open between here and Seward, and we'll be building the new line north from the Matanuska junction and at the same time keep expanding the branch up to the Matanuska coal fields. This will be another busy year."

"Yah sure, da busy hands are goot hands."

A robust smell wafted from the unidentifiable contents of the blackened pan that was placed before the hungry men. Many of the new dishes were altered versions of familiar fare. The stew was now called goulash and the contents remained a mystery. The offerings were generally tasty, but today's spread was worrisome. The men were too hungry to retreat but no one was bold enough to strike first. The bravest among them finally asked, "You gonna tell us what's in this?"

"Braunschweiger," said Hans again, beaming.

"Moose liver sausage," said the fat cook who now preferred to be called le chef. "Lightly seasoned and served with a fine mustard-based sauce."

Mac scooped a less than man-sized portion on to his plate and when he slowly began to eat the others bravely followed. "Any of you fellas heard of Moose Liver Johnson?" he asked as the men tentatively began eating. His tablemates answered with silent stares, at him and at their plates.

"There were a bunch of stories about old Moose Liver back in the early days. Some said he was crazy when he got to Alaska. Others said he was normal when he got here, then got crazier with each passing winter. All agreed that eventually he was one very strange fella."

"Strange how?"

"Well, they say that one year he chased around Fairbanks all winter long with a Mason jar trying to catch the northern lights. Claimed he would be able to light his cabin all winter with just one jar full of those magical dancing lights."

Mac's tablemates listened politely while eating with uncharacteristic caution. Mac set his fork down and continued with his tale. "Then there was the story about the winter he adopted an orphaned moose calf; actually kept that calf in his cabin until it got too big to fit through the door. By then that damn moose would let him ride it like a horse, so he'd ride into Fairbanks on that long-legged critter, wearing a big old cowboy hat and singing those cowboy songs."

"So he had himself an Alaskan horse?"

"That he did, for a while. Then he got to craving moose liver and that was the end of his ride."

"You telling us the truth Mac?"

"Just telling you what I heard."

We finally get January behind us and now the partners are squabbling, thought Mac as he gathered the group around the kitchen table to resolve the dispute over the latest business challenge. "So what are we arguing about today? he asked.

Toot went first. "The railroad's telephone office is planning to print a phone directory and we really need to get a number for the NEW Bunkhouse Royale included in that book."

"And why should we waste money getting a listing in this new phone directory?" asked Jake the bookkeeper.

"So folks will know what number to give to the operator when they want to call the NEW Bunkhouse Royale. They could be customers you know."

Jake looked baffled. "That would make some sense if we had a telephone."

"Well someday we'll be getting a phone and what good will it be to have a damn phone if our number ain't listed in the directory?" asked Toot.

Time to bring this circular discussion to an end, Mac decided. "Like always, you are both part right and part goofy. I'll go talk to the folks at the Telephone Office and see what we can learn about this new book."

Mac and Jake were among the first to tour the new Anchorage hospital that Toot and friends had worked through the winter to complete.

"Why did the railroad build a fancy new hospital?" asked Jake, as they completed their tour of the two-story wood frame building situated on Third Avenue between A and B Streets where it had a commanding view of the rail terminal, harbor and Cook Inlet.

"To provide health care for railroad workers and their families," said Mac.

"Like I've always said, there is plenty to criticize about this government, but there is no denying that they are compassionate. In addition to the base hospital here in Anchorage there are field hospitals along the construction line, and all camps and station contractors are provided with first aid outfits and medicines."

"Is that government compassion the reason why you want to make a career of this railroad job?" asked Jake.

"That's a question I can't quite get my head around," said Mac. *Am I opening a chapter in this book of life that I really don't want to read? Am I really ready to trade my personal freedom for the security of a steady job?*

Toot greeted them at the door of the NEW Bunkhouse Royale. "The Commission's first telephone book is out.

Jake perused the nearly two hundred listings in the new twelve-page book. "I see the NEW Bunkhouse Royale has a number in this book, so now what happens when someone tries to call us?"

"The lady at the Telephone office told me that when we get a phone they will ring us here at the bunkhouse," said Toot. "Until then the operator will just read them a message, like it was from us, saying, 'We're sorry, your call is important to us but we don't have a telephone yet. If you would like to leave a message we'll get back to you when we get a phone.'"

"Hold on just a minute here," said Jake. "The message doesn't match the words."

"You mean that if we really did care about our customers we'd get a phone, and answer it."

"Exactly!"

"Then I reckon we better go ahead and get that new phone ordered."

AEC Railway Yard, March 1, 1917

P.S. Hunt, Alaska Railroad Collection; Anchorage Museum,
B1979.002.AEC.G328

Chapter Twenty-two

Rinnnnng! Rinnnnng! Rinnnnng!

"Yah. Dis is da bunkhouse. You vait now, I vill get Yake."

"Hello, this is Jake at the NEW Bunkhouse Royale. What can I do for you?"

"Hi there partner. Watcha doin!"

"Damn it all to hell Toot! Just because you can use that railroad telephone whenever you want to doesn't mean you need to call me every day just to see what I'm doing! I have work to do you know."

"Gets back to what I just said, watcha doing?"

"I'm getting ready to go see Plumb-bob and find out when we might be able to get our crew back to work. I'd be half way there if I weren't wasting time chatting with you."

"OK, love you too Jake."

"Good Bye." Click!

The March sun and the bright smiles kindled by hints of spring cast a friendly light on the Anchorage that Jake and Sven walked through that morning. Heading down the hill to the rail yards, carefully avoiding both leftover ice and newly minted mud, Jake said, "Ya know Sven, since we got these damn phones all the hell I hear is 'watcha doin,' and I ain't sure anymore if that's a question or a greeting."

"Yah sure," said Sven, then remained deep in thought as they made their way across railroad tracks to the Gee-Oh-Bee.

"Hello boys," said Plumb-bob to Jake and Sven when they strolled into his office, spit-shined and decked out in their spotlessly clean town duds. "Watcha doin?"

Jake shrugged at Sven as if to say, *I'll take that as a question.* Looking at Plumb-bob he said, "Looks like winter has bottomed out, so we're thinking about getting back to work."

"We have survived the depth of the Alaskan winter," said Plumb-bob, "but not the length. We're busy planning work for this construction season but it'll be a few more weeks before we get you back in the field."

"So you will be hiring us back?" asked Jake.

"Contracting work to independent station men produced favorable results last season so we'll be rehiring many of the men when spring arrives. The Damn Yankees were one of our most productive groups so you'll be right at the top of the list."

"We'll have the crew ready," said Jake as they prepared to leave the engineer's office. "Good bye."

"Yah sure," said Sven with sly grin and a small wave. "Vhat-choo-doon."

Mac simply shook his head when Jake asked if they wanted to join up with the Damn Yankees for the summer, but Toot said, "This government carpentering is too good a job to walk away from."

Mac looked at Toot. "Since you like this carpenter work so damn much you ought to try to get on with one of the B & B gangs."

"You mean those Bridge and Buildings folks?" asked Toot. "The ones that build and maintain the railroad's bridges and buildings?"

"Most are being built with native timber so they'll always need upkeep. You get on a B & B gang and you'll have work as long as you want it."

"I got no worries about wanting the work. I'm nervous about this railroad's ability to pay me for the work."

"The Commission is already working on that. The Terminal District here in Anchorage takes over operation and maintenance of the line as soon as a new section is completed, so they can start generating revenue."

"How are they going to create business where their ain't none?" asked Toot.

"The railroad's main strategy is to set up towns at regular intervals along the line. They say these towns will generate traffic, and also provide a safe place for the employees to live."

"Seems like railroad traffic is either there or it ain't."

"Private railroads do this kind of stuff to build business for their companies so this railroad is going to try it too," said Mac.

Toot studied Mac for a moment. "I hope it works."

"Yeah, let's hope so," said Mac. "Eventually the folks in Washington will grow weary of supporting this railroad in Alaska with tax money collected elsewhere, so we'll need revenue to keep this line in business. Right now we haul supplies northward, but I don't see how this perpendicular railroad can be profitable until it has some southbound traffic as well."

"There ain't much of a market for cold air and ice bergs," said Toot, "and I don't know what the hell else we got to be sending south."

"Natural resources, like coal," said Mac. "That was one of the reasons the government decided to build this railroad."

As the spring equinox chased the winter blues from the minds of Anchorage residents the Alaska Engineering Commission confirmed the long-present rumors and posted the new wage scale, to become effective on April 1st.

"Is this some kind of joke?" Toot exclaimed as he burst into the bunkhouse parlor waving a copy of the new wage schedule in front of Mac.

"This is the real thing," said Mac. "The railroad doesn't have a sense of humor. Just coincidence that we get a raise on April Fool's Day."

"I reckon it doesn't matter what day it arrives, as long as we get a raise," said Toot. The men crowded around to get a look at the Revised Wage Schedule.

"The base labor pay goes up to fifty cents per hour," said Jake. "That's a twenty percent increase."

"And carpenters will now get seventy-five cents per hour," said Toot. "Guess I better start looking for one of those B & B jobs."

"Why are there so many rates for cooks?" one of the men asked. "There is one pay rate for all carpenters, one rate for all electricians and one rate for all plumbers, but nine different pay rates for cooks."

Toot grinned and rubbed his stomach. "Makes it easy for us to see what this railroad's priorities are."

I'm as happy as anyone to be getting a raise, thought Mac, watching Toot make a beeline for the coat rail. *But I think we're mistaken if we think we can't ever drink this government well dry.*

Toot donned his coat and hat. "Let's mosey over to one of those edge-of-town places that sell booze and have us a drink."

As the easily convinced men grabbed for their coats one asked, "You going to join us Mac?"

"Believe I will."

Rinnnnng! Rinnnnng! Rinnnnng!

Jake dropped his magazine and ran to the phone. "This is the NEW Bunkhouse Royale; how can I help you?"

"I don't need help Jake; I'm calling to talk to you."

"Toot are you calling to chat again?"

"I'm not calling to chat; I'm calling to give you the big news."

"What news."

"We're going to war," said Toot said. In an instant the excitement that had enveloped Anchorage over pay raises and the upcoming construction season was smothered by the news that on April 6, 1917 the United States declared war on Germany.

SS Turret Crown at Anchorage

P.S. Hunt, Alaska Railroad Collection; Anchorage Museum,
B1979.002.AEC.G466

Chapter Twenty-three

As Commissioner Mears watched crews unload railway equipment from the steamer *Turret Crown,* just arrived from Panama, Mac asked, "Your mind is on the war these days I expect?"

"I'm conflicted, Mac. I'm as committed to building this railroad as I've ever been to anything in my entire life, and things are going very well. The project is gaining momentum, Anchorage is thriving, the Ship Creek rail yards are established and trains are operating over the completed segments of the line. But, I am a career Army man and my country is now at war."

They watched silently as a giant 200-class locomotive was gently lowered on to the awaiting track, then Mac turned to his boss. "And I'm certain that being a family man makes it all very personal for you."

"That, my friend, is what makes this decision so absolutely gut-wrenching. My wife just gave birth to our fourth child, and I'm certainly not anxious to leave my family behind while I'm off in France for months or years, or perhaps forever. On the other hand, I certainly don't want my kids to grow up thinking of me as one who shirked his duty."

"That's why it will be easier for unattached men, like us railroad workers, to go off to fight this war. Do you think the government will even continue with the railroad building, with a war on and all?"

"We're too far along to stop this project now," said Mears with a confidence that calmed Mac's uneasiness. When Mears also said, "but it's now more important than ever to start generating revenue," Mac's apprehensions reasserted themselves.

"Seems like we could make big money shipping coal," said Mac. The need to transport men and materials to France will certainly increase the demand for coal."

"It will, and Alaskan coal could help meet that need, if we were ready. Unfortunately, even though congress told us to build a rail line to the coal fields, they haven't made us responsible for mining coal, or appropriated any money to develop the coal mining facilities."

"And we still haven't figured out how to get the coal loaded on ships," said Mac. "The port here in Anchorage is too shallow. But, it doesn't make sense to haul heavy loads of coal another hundred miles over the mountains to Seward."

Mears watched as the last of the six big locomotives was safely unloaded. "This is the most logical place to export Alaskan coal from, but that will require improving the port here in Anchorage. Of course Mr. Ballaine disagrees, and is organizing the opposition."

"He's been upset since the Commission's headquarters was relocated from Seward to Anchorage, hasn't he?"

"Oh yes! Moving Commissioner Edes and other railroad staff up to Anchorage ruined his plans to sells his Seward lots to the railroad at inflated prices. He is even more upset now, so he has the Seward business community mounting an effort to get Seward designated as the preferred coal loading port."

"Will he succeed?" asked Mac.

"Not this time. We're already moving ahead with plans to dredge the port here in Anchorage."

"I reckon that's what Poetic Pete's latest verse is all about."

We can't load our coal cuz of that shoal,
That's made of Cook Inlet mud.
For a coal-filled boat will no longer float,
When it's stuck in that awful crud.

"Can't make the water higher, so the bottom we'll lower,"
Said the men of the engineer corps.
"We'll build a machine that's part submarine,
And dig a hole in the ocean floor."

They had an old barge, a hundred-forty feet large,
That someone had named the SPERM.
"'Tis a floating sled," the engineers said,
"A platform for our mud-sucking worm."

"We'll add a boiler and a big generator,
To power that mighty pump.
The sea floor it'll eat, down seventy-five feet,
And on shore the mud she'll dump."

So that dredge was built to mine the silt,
And off the bow a cutterhead hung,
Where it'd suck up ocean floor, to be sent ashore,
Through the giant pipe they'd strung.

The dredge was ready and the crowd was giddy,
As they cheered and watched with glee.
But when the switch was thrown there was a mighty groan,
For the shore was pumped to the sea!

Mears smiled now. "I'm confident this guy Gerig, that I've hired to manage the dredging operation, will get it right. I knew him in Panama and he's a bright man who knows how to get things done. For now, we need to focus on this construction season."

"We still plan to get the line open up to Montana Creek before winter don't we?" asked Mac.

"We do, but to do that we need to get the bridge across the Little Susitna finished, and the information I'm getting says they're behind schedule."

Mac worked his way north from Anchorage, tracking first northeast before curving around the head of Knik Arm and then heading northwest across the Matanuska-Susitna Valley. Surrounded by the Alaska, Talkeetna and Chugach mountains the vast glacier-formed Mat-Su Valley is drained by rivers and streams that are the spawning grounds for several species of salmon. Sixty miles up the rail line, but only thirty miles due north of Anchorage, he came to the Little Susitna River. Mac took a long look at the bridge construction, or lack of construction. He shook hands with the foreman. "We expected this bridge to be near done by now."

"That may be what you expected, but it ain't what yer getting. If the bosses in Anchorage wanted this bridge sooner they should have gotten us started sooner. Why the hell should we bust our asses to make up for their mistakes?"

Mac rested his long burly arms on his hips. "They can't start the work until they get the money from Washington."

"Screw ups from the bosses, whether in Washington or Anchorage, ain't my problem—"

Mac cut him off. "But it is your problem! All of us need to be thinking about what we can do to get this railroad built. At the rate this bridge is coming together the rail gang will be here before you're done, then the entire project will be off schedule."

The foreman puffed up and raised his voice now. "Maybe this will teach them a lesson."

"That type of attitude will—"

"I'm drawing good pay and the longer it takes to get this bridge built the more I make. Why should I give a damn about the railroad's problems?"

Mac spat out the words now, overpowering the man's attempts to interrupt. "Because others are trying to make a living here too. This railroad goes out of its way to take good care of us workers, but they expect us to work. Your self-centered focus will kill the goose that feeds us all. That hourly pay rate you're so damn proud of, when multiplied times zero, comes out to zero."

The foreman's eyes were still talking as Mac marched away, but his mouth remained tightly shut.

Funny how time speeds up when things slow down, thought Mac. He watched the days fly by while the bridge progress numbers moved sluggishly. *Driven by the apathetic attitude of one foreman.*

Mac's fears were confirmed in early June when the northbound track work ground to a halt at the still unfinished bridge. The setback frustrated Mr. Mears and taught Mac yet another railroading lesson. *The weather works against us, the land works against us, the government works against us and sometimes we even stumble over our own feet.*

Baseball Excursion Train to Potter

P.S. Hunt, Alaska Railroad Collection; Anchorage Museum,
B1979.002.AEC.G588

Chapter Twenty-four

"All aboard," the conductor called on a delightful Sunday morning as the baseball players and fans anxiously clambered aboard the open top rail cars, quickly filling them to capacity, standing room only. July is a glorious month in Anchorage, perhaps the best of the twelve, and everyone was anxious to start this one with the baseball game pitting the Anchorage team against the men of Turnagain Arm. The railroad voiced their support for wholesome off-duty activity by running the excursion train to Potter, the venue for the big game.

Mac enjoyed the boisterous players and fans, happy to be part of the celebration. Rounding the point below the bluff the train headed south, quickly leaving the new city behind. All talk was of baseball as they traveled through the wooded countryside south of Anchorage, but the group grew silent when they reached the shore of Turnagain Arm. Skirting along the water's edge they remained dumbstruck, captivated now by the spectacular view of the estuary and the surrounding mountains decked out in their summer green.

Potter, clinging to any available land between the sharply rising face of the Chugach and the Turnagain mud flats, was overrun by Anchorage fans as the train cars were offloaded. The players made their way to the improvised diamond while Mac and the other fans strolled through the railroad camp. The celebrative young men patronized the bootlegger's cabin in the woods near the camp before returning to the ball park to watch the teams warm up.

The umpire yelled, "PLAY BALL."

Mac and his friends said, "here's mud in your eye." Then, as their star player stepped up to bat they yelled, "TIFF-AH-NEE! TIFF-AH-NEE!"

To the delight of the visiting fans F.W. Tiffany and the balance of the Anchorage team soon took the lead. By the time a late inning hit soared over the head of the Potter outfielder and disappeared into the Cook Inlet mud the celebration was already underway.

"Swing," said the Potter manager to the batter who'd watched a pitch sail by untouched. "Nobody ever hit a homerun watching the ball." Following his advice, the batter took a mighty swing, and the hardwood bat missed the ball but connected squarely with the nose of the Anchorage star. The game ended with Anchorage ahead five to one, but the Potter team left the field with nine unbroken noses.

Late that afternoon the train rumbled slowly through the remote area that Anchorage would one day consume while the players and fans recounted the exciting game. "Too bad Toot couldn't make the trip with us," said Mac to one of the men.

"He sure does love baseball, but since he got that B & B job he's been working out of town much of the time."

"The glitch up at the Little Su worked out good for him," said Mac. "Pressure to complete the bridge created openings on the Bridge and Buildings gang and Toot got the job that he'd been waiting for, but he won't have time for baseball this summer."

As the train approached Ship Creek the man handed the bottle to Mac. "Can't have booze in town, so we better drain this now."

Back in town Mac walked slowly back to the bunkhouse, his normally robust stride now erratic.

"The gap between here and Seward isn't closing nearly as fast as I'd like," said Mears as he and Mac reviewed the summer progress reports. Mac mulled over the numbers, and in his head counted the remaining months available before freeze-up. "We're making progress from both ends but it doesn't look like we'll get the gap closed this summer. It's slow going along those rocky slopes."

"I know. The work is just too difficult and too dangerous to be rushed. We may not join the lines this year, but I want to narrow that gap as much as absolutely possible."

"At least the track gang up north is moving again, now that the bridge over the Little Su is open."

"Didn't take long to get it finished, once we got a new foreman."

"Why did the government buy that bankrupt rail line?" asked Mac when he heard that the Commission had paid $300,000 to purchase the forty-four-mile-long narrow-gauge Tanana Valley Railroad. "The price seems reasonable enough, but declining gold mining operations have left the line profitless."

"Mostly because we get seven miles of right-of-way from Happy on into Fairbanks," said Mears. "We also get needed facilities and rail yards in Fairbanks, and their Chena and Chatanika branches will provide feeder lines that will bring traffic into our main system when it is completed."

"But it is a narrow gauge line. Our equipment won't work on that three-foot wide track."

"True," said Mears, "but it can be converted to standard gauge when the rest of our system is completed. Until then we can utilize the narrow gauge equipment to support construction activities."

That evening, Mac explained the railroad's plans for the Tanana Valley line to his friends at the bunkhouse dinner table and then broke the most intriguing news of the day. "Guess what Jake and his crew found up by Dead Horse Hill?"

"Another bear?" asked one of the residents. A track crew had recently been forced to kill a large brown bear that had attacked one of the crew members and the story had quickly been added to the growing list of bear encounter tales.

"Nope, not another bear story," said Mac, then returned to his dinner.

One of the hungry men finally paused just long enough to ask, "Well what then?"

"They found a message carved in a tree up by mile 245, left there years ago by an Alaska Central survey crew."

The eating stopped now. Then one asked, "What sort of message?"

"Just said, MAY WE NEVER RETURN, and listed the names of the crew. And, who do you think was on that crew?"

There were blank stares the table around, curious. Mac hesitated, slowly looked face to face to face, and then finally answered his own question. "Moose Liver Johnson."

Station Gang Along Turnagain Arm, November, 1917

Alaska Railroad Collection; Anchorage Museum,
B1979.002.AEC.H22

Chapter Twenty-five

Fall passed in the customary beautiful but brief flash of color and by late October the rapidly descending snowline on the mountains north of Talkeetna ended the Damn Yankee's brush clearing season. Traveling south toward Anchorage they passed the new LAKE NANCY sign that had been erected by the picturesque lake at mile 180 of the new rail line.

"Hoo da hell is Nan Cee?" asked Sven.

"The daughter of the Secretary of the Interior, Franklin Lane," said Jake in a disparaging tone, casting an equally disparaging glance toward the sign."

"Dis lake should have da name of dat Alaska person, Moose Living Yohnson."

"Aye, ne, da, ja!"

The Damn Yankees watched attentively as Jake dealt the cards.

"Five cards. Face up. High hand gets first bath; second highest hand gets second bath, and on down the line until you are all clean." After weeks of bathing in cold streams the men were happy to be back in the comfortable bunkhouse and anxious for the luxury of a hot bath. Their clothes were washed and boiled and washed and boiled again until the coarse work wear was as presentable as the banker's suit on Sunday morning.

The sun-darkened faces of the lean yet muscular men joined the regulars at the communal table that evening, anxious to reacquaint themselves with the fat cook's cuisine.

"Yumpin yiminney!" Sven yelled as the bunkhouse floor took a jump, and the smiles disappeared from the Damn Yankee's clean-shaven faces. As the entire building moved side to side the faces circling the table instantly went from jovial banter to wordless panic.

Alaska's location along the circum-Pacific rim gives her more earthquakes than the rest of the United States combined so Mac was quite accustomed to the tremblors, but his stomach knotted when yet another sharp jolt shot from deep underground, passing through the building and the men. The surreal experience of watching water-like waves flow through the solid earth outside the window produced an instant trance, and the uncertainty as to how severe the quake would be filled his head with images of falling buildings and gaping man-eating chasms in the earth.

The cupboards rattled as though the dishes were suddenly trying to escape. The panicked look on the men's faces mirrored Mac's concerns. When the noise and ground movement stopped the men started breathing again, though the overhead lamp continued to sway. The knowledge that they had survived yet another quake brought relief but they remained silent. Eventually Sven spoke for the entire crew, "Ve should be making da tracks dat go away from dis place."

Jake got up and looked around, checking for damage and regaining his composure. "There are earthquakes in every corner of Alaska, so we can't hide from them, but I do have an idea."

"Yah," said Sven, as ten eyes focused on Jake.

"Plumb-bob tells me the railroad is continuing station work along Turnagain Arm this winter. At least then we'd be living in a canvas house so it won't hurt much if it falls on us during an earthquake."

"Vhy do dey vant us to verk in da cold time?" asked Sven.

"I don't think they want to work in the cold, but they do want to get the line connected between here and Seward by next summer and that won't happen unless they get the rock cleared this winter," said Jake. "It'll be hard work, dangerous, and cold, and we'll also have to deal with the short days. But, we'll be getting paid."

"Yah sure, and da long nights are goot for da poker playing."

"Aye, ne, da, ja!"

The Damn Yankees lay in their bed rolls repeating, "brr, brrr, brrrr," the universal word for, "would someone please get up and build a fire." An early November storm was inflicting misery on them and the other contractors clearing rock south of Bird Point, roughly midway down the northern edge of Turnagain Arm. The sub-zero weather and heavy snow piled slush ice five feet high on the mud flats.

"Dis snow and cold makes me sick to be home at dat shaky bunkhouse," said Sven as he reluctantly crawled out to rekindle their stove.

The hard-working crew spent the cold, dark and short winter days clearing away rock mountainsides to create a flat railbed along Turnagain Arm. The rail alignment zigged left and then zagged right as it made its way along the edge of the estuary, and while horizontal zigging and zagging was acceptable, vertical zigzags were completely unacceptable. Dynamite and steam shovels were used where possible, but much of the work was done by station gangs.

Each night after they'd thawed and eaten Sven would say, "time for da poker," as they headed off to the evening game in a nearby tent. When they returned the number of smiling faces was generally matched by the number of frowns.

"It's just numbers," said Jake. "Your odds are exactly the same as everyone else in the game, so over time it all evens out. What you win tonight you lose tomorrow night."

"Unless you are da better player."

"Everyone in the game thinks he is the best player; why else would he play? Just remember that you're playing with friends out here at camp, but back in town there are those who swing the odds in their favor by cheating. And be damn sure you don't get in debt to those town goons. Do that and you'll end up doing the dead-man's float in Cook Inlet."

"Aye, yah sure, ne, da, ja!"

"And, while you were out giving away your money I got the latest news from Anchorage."

"Vas der any goot news?"

"Well, rumor has it that someone took down the railroad's sign at Nancy Lake and put up a new sign."

"Ya sure. Vhat das dat nuu sign say?"

"Well, it's now Moose Liver Johnson Lake."

AEC Employees Leave for Military Service

H.G. Kaiser, Alaska Railroad Collection; Anchorage Museum,
B1979.002.AEC.G863

Chapter Twenty-six

"War news is bad again," said Mac as he read the newspaper in the bunkhouse parlor. The freshly painted room was again a warm and cozy refuge from the deepening winter, but most of the chairs surrounding the stove were empty now.

Toot looked up from the magazine on his lap. "Ain't no such thing as good war news you know."

"You're right about that. I expect that's why we're seeing so much patriotism clear up here in Alaska. Folks are supporting the Interior Department's War Relief Bureau, the Red Cross and even the Soldiers Tobacco Fund."

"We also sent those sets of baseball equipment to the boys in France. Hope they get a chance to use them."

Mac's lack of expression exposed his feelings when he said, "The most personal commitment comes from the railroaders who enlisted in the Army."

"And now they're fixin' to start drafting men too. I hear the Anchorage Registration Board has already assigned numbers to over two thousand men."

"They have, and they've put them in five classes. Those in Class I will be the first called to service and many railroad workers are at the top of that class; single men without dependent relatives. They also put married men in Class I if they habitually fail to support their family, depend on their wife for support, or are not working."

"You have nothing to worry about, Mac. You got no wife to neglect."

"I'm too old to be drafted," said Mac, "but I worry about the rest of you. And if this war uses up all the money in Washington there won't be any left for this railroad. And if there are no men in Anchorage we won't have any customers here at the bunkhouse."

The look in Toot's eyes confirmed his fear. "Enough worries to drive a man to drink."

"I'm afraid it already has," said Mac, "and I'm worried about that too."

"Maybe you need to take up bowling. They're organizing clubs for a winter bowling tournament at the YMCA alleys. You ought to find a girlfriend and join one of those teams."

"The hourly rate for girlfriends in this town would make that bowling real expensive," said Mac. "But I am glad to see that people are getting ready for winter. Judging from the size of that pile of stolen magazines it's going to be a long one."

Ignoring the mid-December cold, Mac joined about fifty Anchorage Chamber of Commerce members and guests departing Anchorage on a special excursion train to Potter Creek. Commissioner Mears and District Engineer Fredrick Hansen were personally conducting the tour. Mac knew that Mears' thoughts were likely elsewhere since his recent promotion to the rank of Major in the regular Army clearly meant that he would soon be leaving his post in Alaska to join the war effort.

The town's leading citizens rode through previously untracked land in comfortable day coaches pulled over a steel rail system by a steam-powered locomotive. The transformation of Alaska had begun and like the weighty locomotive, once moving, was largely unstoppable.

As the train rumbled through the spectacular winter-scape Mac joined the group congregated around Mears in the open observation car despite the twenty-five below zero temperature. All listened politely as the Commissioner recounted the year's progress.

"We had as many as forty-five hundred men working on the project this year and except for the roughly twenty-mile gap along Turnagain Arm the line is open from Seward up to Anchorage and ninety-four miles northward to Montana Creek, and there are branch lines to the coal mines in the Matanuska Valley. Right-of-way has been cleared and graded beyond the end of steel, and significant bridge work has been done. Crews up north are moving south from Nenana, and we've purchased the Tanana Valley Railroad, providing an instant rail line from Happy up to Fairbanks."

"Is the line generating revenue yet?" asked one of the businessmen.

"Yes it is," said Mears. "We operate the completed portions of the rail system as a revenue-producing rail company. Income for this year will exceed sixty thousand dollars."

At Potter Creek the excursionists were served lunch at the Commission mess hall before the return trip. When they got off the train back in Anchorage at mid-afternoon Mac fell in step with Mears as they made their way across the already dark rail yard. He knew that his job was in jeopardy as the Commissioner prepared to leave for the Army, but until then he remained dedicated to the man who, to Mac's way of thinking, was the person most responsible for the success of the Alaskan railway project.

"What's on your mind, Mac?" asked Mears, "besides this cold weather."

"We are having a bit of a cold spell," said Mac. "But mostly I've been wondering what next year may bring."

"Next year will be much different than this year was."

"For the railroad, sir? Or for you?"

"Both."

HIGH IRON TO FAIRBANKS

PART FOUR
The War Years
(1918 - 1919)

COL. P. MEARS E.E.C. LEAVING ANCHORAGE ALASKA FOR WASHINGTON & THE WAR-FRONT.

Mears Family Leaving Anchorage

Chapter Twenty-seven

"My family and I will be leaving Anchorage on Saturday," said Mears when Mac walked into the office on the first workday of 1918.

Mac took a deep breath and asked, "A one-way trip?"

"Afraid so. I've been authorized to recruit a railroad construction regiment to serve in France and I'm heading back to Washington to meet with War Department officials."

Mac's feet stuck to the floor. He'd long expected that Mears would be leaving but the abruptness of the announcement unleashed a flood of anxiety. When his blood pressure returned to the normal range he said, "I'd be honored to serve in your new regiment sir, if you'll have me."

"I will certainly need experienced railroaders but I don't want to take men away from this project unless I have to, and they need you here Mac. Andy Christensen will be responsible for the Anchorage Division until my replacement is named, and I've promised him that you'll be here to help him."

"If that's what you want, sir, that's what I'll do," said Mac, but at the same time wondered, *but what'll happen to my job when the real new boss gets here?* Before he could put the question to words Mears answered.

"I'd hope that my permanent replacement will keep you on too, but of course that will be up to him."

So I now have a temporary job working for the temporary new boss, thought Mac as he sauntered out of the room.

Mac was still brooding as he strolled into the Anchorage Labor Temple the following evening to attend the hastily arranged farewell party for Frederick and Jane Mears.

"Evening," he said to the already seated guests as he squeezed into the last empty chair at the long table, deliberately picking a spot near the rear where he could remain anonymous. His table mates tried to include him in their conversation but he made little effort to join what he saw as all-too-festive chatter. Despite the January cold the over-stoked stove and the three-hundred souls crowded into the hall pushed the temperature to a level that added to Mac's discomfort.

The crowd grew quiet when the master of ceremonies stood to speak. "On behalf of all of us here tonight I want to say thank you to Major Mears for giving us a town that we can be proud of." He politely waited for the applause to subside, then said, "and a special thank you to Mrs. Mears for all she has done to promote education in our town." Everyone in the hall watched attentively as more accolades and gifts were bestowed upon Mr. and Mrs. Mears.

Mac silently approved when Andrew Christensen spoke. After acknowledging Mears' accomplishments and pointing out that he would have done much more if he hadn't been limited by federal funding problems, Christensen said, "The people of Anchorage have a gift for you. We couldn't get it made on such short notice but we do have a picture." The crowd cheered loudly when Christensen presented Mears with a picture of a ceremonial cavalry saber etched in gold, with the initials FM embedded with diamonds.

Mears stood. "Jane and I thank you, one and all, for these special gifts, which we shall cherish forever." Mac thought he saw Mears glance his way when he said, "These gifts will always remind us of the friendships we have been blessed with here in Anchorage."

The Major talked of the work already done before saying, "We can all be proud of what we have accomplished in the short time that we've been here, but we're not done, so the work will go on."

The crowd was focused when the toastmaster joined Mears at the podium and raised his glass. "A toast to Major Mears, the man who gave us Anchorage."

"To Major Mears," the crowd said, raising their glasses.

"To Major Mears, the man who built the railroad."

"To Major Mears!"

"To Major Mears, the man who brought us Jane Mears!"

The crowd stood now, applauding loudly.

Mac joined the others who stepped outside to smoke and drink while the tables were cleared away to make room for dancing. As he stood in the cold lamenting Mears' departure he watched a group of railroad managers congregate around Mr. Christensen. *They could at least wait for one boss to get out of town before they start toadying to the new boss*, thought Mac. When he heard another group of administrative staff making plans to occupy the railroad residence the Mears family was vacating Mac moved away, frustrated.

After the brief exposure to the cold Alaskan night the overheated hall felt good to Mac, but as the dancing started his ever observant gaze confirmed that once again the women in attendance were far outnumbered by the men. Anchorage's male to female ratio was still seriously unbalanced, Mac knew, and it was even worse in the outlying communities. The recent Christmas dance up at Dead Horse Hill had been attended by forty men and four women.

Snow was falling confetti-like from the gray Alaskan sky when Mac joined the crowd gathered at the Anchorage Depot the next morning. As he watched the Mears family board the train Mac waved and silently said his good-bye to the man who had changed his life. *Wonder why we say good bye at times like this* he thought, *when there's not a damn thing good about these partings. I may never see this man again. And, without his leadership this project may falter.*

"The fire started about four o'clock this morning." Andrew Christensen said to Mac when he reported to work on a mid-January morning. Christensen was sitting behind the desk that Mac, still accustomed to Mears, considered too big for him. The temporary boss clutched the just received telegram, a troubled look on his face. "Completely destroyed the round house in Nenana, along with all of the standard gauge locomotives."

"Trouble piled on top of trouble up on the north end," said Mac. Just a few miles south of town the Nenana River had tired of its traditional channel the prior fall, as rivers sometimes do, and poured through an overflow known as Lost Slough, threatening the newly constructed rail line. "I'm told that all of their efforts to invite the river back to original form have been unsuccessful."

"Totally unsuccessful," said Christensen. "Several miles of railroad will have to be abandoned and rebuilt on higher ground." Then, pulling another piece of paper from the already cluttered desk, "At least there is some good news. We received this telegram from Secretary Lane announcing the appointment of William Gerig as engineer-in-charge of the Anchorage division. He's down in the States on leave so I'll be in charge until he gets back up here."

"I'm sure he'll be back soon," said Mac.

"Not soon enough for me. I'm already weary of dealing with Washington and the pressure right now isn't about building this railroad, it's about supporting the war effort. Seems like all I get are new directions on conserving food."

When Mac returned home from work that evening Toot was already busy shoveling snow from the bunkhouse sidewalk. "You must be fighting a case of cabin fever," said Mac. "There's hardly enough snow there to bother with."

"We don't want to pay the damn railroad to shovel it for us. They told the businesses over on Fourth Avenue that if they didn't keep the snow cleared they would charge them to have it shoveled. Don't you guys at the Gee-Oh-Bee have better things to worry about, like building a railroad?"

"No one is thinking much about railroad building these days, just fussing about saving food," said Mac to his snow-shoveling partner. "Food will win the war. That's what they're saying."

"I'm thinking soldiers will win the war."

"I agree with you on that," said Mac. "But they're serious about this food conservation stuff. They say the country needs food to support the soldiers, so they're starting a major effort to get folks to eat less. They want everyone in Anchorage to sign cards pledging to observe meatless Tuesdays and Fridays, wheat-less Wednesdays and pork-less Saturdays."

Toot leaned on his shovel and looked quizzically at his partner. "I ain't sure how changing our eating schedule will change the amount of food folks are eating, but I reckon nothing changes here at the bunkhouse unless they ask us to observe moose-less Mondays."

"Actually," said Mac, "they want us to eat more wild game. They're trying to change game laws to allow Alaskans to kill more wild game for food."

"Seems like we already eat plenty of wild game," said Toot, "but we sure as hell need to save some money. With all these empty bunks the money is going out the door faster than it's coming in."

Mac furrowed his brows. "The bunkhouse and the railroad are both struggling right now."

A new boss is always a worrisome thing so during the long nights of the short month of February Mac laid awake arguing with himself.

Maybe this new boss will be as good to me as Mr. Mears was.

That ain't likely! Think about it, has anyone else ever treated me this well?

Well no. But Mr. Mears spoke highly of this new guy, Gerig.

Good luck runs in streaks you know, and it's about time for this streak to be running out.

NO! I'm determined to break that cycle.

Why should I believe that? We've never succeeded before.

How are we going to resolve this standoff?

Can't. We're talking to our self.

I keep forgetting that.

Me too.

"You look like you haven't slept in a month," a coworker said one morning when Mac showed up at the railroad looking totally wrung out. "You on the bottle again?"

"I have a drink now and then, but mostly I lay awake at night worrying that my job will end when Mr. Gerig gets here. I was really hoping to make this railroad job last."

"You'll still be here, Mac; Government already said so."

"Said what?" asked Mac.

"I saw the General Circular right from the Department of the Interior, signed by Commissioner Edes. Said that effective January 1st William Gerig was Engineer-in-Charge of the Anchorage Division."

"Gerig wasn't even here on January 1st."

"Doesn't matter. The important thing is that the Circular also said folks 'heretofore' reporting to Commissioner Mears will 'hereafter' report to Mr. Gerig. You'll still have your job, Mac."

The happy cloud that followed Mac around the balance of the day accompanied him up the hill to Anchorage that evening, and then led him straight to his favorite watering hole.

"The usual?" the barkeep asked as Mac entered the dingy back room of an equally dingy establishment.

"Make it a double," said Mac. "I need to toast my new job."

"Thought you already had a job."

"I do, and now I get to keep it."

Later, on the walk home Mac realized that even the cold air could not clear the fog from his pickled brain. When he staggered into the bunkhouse Toot was sitting in the parlor.

"Mac, we need to find you a gal friend to keep you warm so you won't need so damn much antifreeze. Too much boozin' ain't good for a person. You in particular!"

"I know" said Mac, struggling to find the buttons on his coat.

William Gerig (left) and Mrs. Gerig Arrive in Anchorage

H.G. Kaiser, Alaska Railroad Collection; Anchorage Museum,
B1979.002.AEC.G860

Chapter Twenty-eight

"We will not let this project be derailed." William Gerig said to Mac when he returned to Anchorage and took the reins of the Anchorage Division. "The war will slow our progress but we will continue building this railroad."

This new boss seems determined to fill Mear's shoes, Mac observed, before saying, "The rocky slopes along Turnagain Arm are slowing us down right now; but we should get the line between here and Seward connected this summer, with a little luck."

"Luck hell!" Gerig yelled, with I'm damn serious written all over his face. "We'll get it done with hard work."

The intensity of the retort caught Mac off guard. He knew that Mr. Gerig was a seasoned construction manager who had helped build the Panama Railroad, and he now understood that like others of that calling Gerig didn't take no, or even maybe, for an answer.

Before Mac could untangle his tongue Gerig said, "Damn it, we won't be intimidated by a few rivers and mountains."

Mac took a moment to get his self-doubt under control, then said exactly what he was thinking. "I don't believe rivers and mountains will be our problem. My concern is that we'll run out of workers. The war itself will draw many railroaders away, and our funding uncertainties will chase away a bunch more. These young men will disappear just as quickly as they appeared, and we can't build this railroad without them."

Gerig maintained his no-nonsense demeanor, but spoke at a normal decibel level when he said, "I like a man that says what's on his mind, and what you say makes sense. In a building full of experts on what happened last year it's nice to have someone looking beyond the next bend."

With their winter contract work along Turnagain Arm completed Jake and the crew moved back to the comfort of the NEW Bunkhouse Royale, a warm building with real beds and real walls.

The mood at the bunkhouse was upbeat as Jake and his crew made plans for their winter's pay. Then Toot said, "I hate to piss on your fire, but you men ought to worry less about your money and start paying attention to those draft numbers the government assigned to you. What I'm hearing is that by the end of June about seven hundred Alaskans will be drafted."

As the faces turned serious Jake eyed Mac and asked, "Is this true?"

"I know that this draft threat has men disappearing left and right," said Mac.

"That's a fact," said Toot. "Some join the Army and others just disappear."

The mood in the room took another step backwards when Mac said, "Many railroaders will be getting drafted. Jake's eyesight will make him ineligible, and the Army sure as hell won't take Hans, with him being a German, but the rest of you are exactly what the Army is looking for."

"Except for Sven," said Toot, "he was already rejected."

"How the hell did he get rejected?" asked Jake.

"We stopped by that Army office this afternoon," said Toot, "and they asked him, 'Do you want to volunteer for service in the United States Army. So Sven, he said 'Yah Sure.'"

"Then the Army guy stepped right up to his face and yelled, "Did you mean YES, SIR?"

"Then Sven said, 'Yah sure, you bettcha,' and that Army guy kicked his ass out the door. Said, 'We got no room for wise guys in this Army.'"

The laughter faded away when Mac said, "You'll be called according to your draft number, starting with number one, so the future of you other men will be determined by that number on your draft card. Mac's concern grew as the men compared the numbers on the cards that had been sent to them by the Registration Board and found that Toot and Paddy had low draft numbers. The angst-ridden men were in deep discussion when Mac slipped away and went to bed.

Jake was at the table working on his second cup of coffee when Mac returned to the kitchen early the next morning. "You been here all night, or are you up early?"

"Couldn't sleep. The boys and I sat up late talking about this draft stuff; how it will affect each of them, and what will become of this station man business we have going."

Mac poured a cup of coffee and sat at the table. "It'd be a shame to break up your crew."

Jake's somber expression telegraphed the gravity of his message. "The boys believe this country has been good to them and they want to be good back, so Oleg and Kosta have decided to volunteer for the Army."

"But Toot and Paddy will be the first ones drafted," said Mac. "They have the low draft numbers."

Jake's eye looked deadly serious now. "That's where this plan gets complicated. Oleg and Kosta don't want Toot and Paddy to get drafted, so they're going to serve in their place."

"What the hell do you mean, that Oleg and Kosta will sign up as Toot and Paddy?"

"Nope, they'll use their own names, but they are going to use Toot's and Paddy's draft numbers. That way those numbers can't ever come up again."

"Won't the Army check?"

"Why would they check? They sure as hell won't be expecting anyone to use the wrong draft number."

Mac was baffled now. "But what will happen later on, when they call Oleg and Kosta's numbers for the draft and find out they're in the Army?"

"They'll probably figure they made a mistake. But the Army is like Nigel, they may make mistakes but they'll never admit to one. And, they can't draft men who are already in the Army can they?"

Mac went to the stove, grabbed a rag to hold the hot coffee pot and brought it back to the table. With the cups refilled he said, "I admire what these men are trying to do, but I wonder how Oleg and Kosta will get in the Army when they don't speak much English yet?"

Jake cleared that up. "This is a shooting war, not a talking war, and nobody can shoot better than Oleg and Kosta."

Before the week was out Oleg and Kosta were in line at the Army induction center. When Oleg reached the front of the queue he gave his name to the uniformed soldier sitting at the typing machine. When asked for his draft registration number Oleg slowly recited the number assigned to Toot and no questions were asked. Kosta stepped up and repeated the process, and gave them Paddy's draft number. Two numbers were crossed off the list, never to be used again.

The railroad is overrun by questions, thought Mac as he made his way across town on the morning of the spring equinox, the Chugach glistening in the background. *Who will be going off to war next? Will railroad construction continue? Is the tide turning again?* The question that popped out when he got to Mr. Gerig's office was, "Is it true that some railroad folks have been given permission to join Major Mears' railroad regiment?"

"It's Colonel Mears now," said Gerig. "The new regiment is being mobilized at Fort Leavenworth in Kansas and some railroaders plan to join him but they still have to get approval from Commissioner Edes."

Mac shrugged. "But he hasn't been seen around here for a while."

"Edes is still back in Washington."

"Well, it is important to keep the government money flowing," said Mac. "And, I expect that means somebody has to kowtow to the folks back east."

"True enough," said Gerig, "but it seems there is no end to it. Our highest mountain is named after a dead president who never set foot in Alaska. Now the folks up in Nenana named their new elementary school after Interior Secretary Lane and we already named that lake after his daughter. Pretty soon everything up here in Alaska is going to be named after some self-adoring politician."

As they turned their attention to the March numbers report Gerig said, "Looks like you were right. We lost almost one fourth of our employees in the first quarter of this year."

"Not a good way to start the year."

"And we're not only losing our workers, we're losing our Commissioners too. President Wilson has nominated Tom Riggs to be governor of the Territory of Alaska and with Mears off in the Army the Alaska Engineering Commission is now a committee of one, and he spends all his time back in Washington."

"Hell of a way to build a railroad!"

Railroad Construction Camp at Goldstream, April 1918

Chapter Twenty-nine

Hans casually glanced at the three jacks in his hand and at the stoic faces of the other men sitting around the table in the smoky room. There was a large pile of cash in front of him for his luck had run strong all night. Wordlessly, he pushed it all to the center of the table. The faces and voices in the room stilled when the bearded man across the table reached in his vest pocket and pulled out a small poke, shook out a gold nugget and placed it atop the pile of money and said, "I'll call." When the man turned over three aces Hans slowly got to his feet, tipped his hat and left the table.

"So he's lost all his money?" asked Mac at the breakfast table the next morning, where the conversation centered on Hans' big poker loss.

Hans looked on as Jake explained. "He has some seed money. He figures that way he can go win back the money he lost."

To change the subject to something more palatable Mac said, "You men remember that the government directed everyone to set their watches ahead one hour, precisely at midnight tonight." Daily routines in pre-railroad Alaska were often governed by weather, available daylight, salmon runs and caribou migrations. Some Alaskans had accepted the structure dictated by the railroad's need for schedules, but judging from the looks that he got from the men at the bunkhouse breakfast table Mac knew they did not embrace the idea that time would somehow be saved if, on the opening second of April Fool's Day in 1918, everyone advanced their clocks by one hour.

"It's true," said Mac. "The Congress passed what they call a Daylight Saving bill, and the President approved."

"How does setting our watches ahead save daylight?" asked Jake.

Toot smirked. "Makes about as much sense as that crazy old Moose Liver Johnson trying to put northern lights in a Mason jar."

Mac could think of no argument. "Kind of the same thing I reckon."

"Why the hell doesn't the government forget all this craziness and get back to railroad building?" asked Jake.

"We are going to," said Mac. "President Wilson himself told congress that they ought to continue with the construction."

"Well the boys and I are agreeing with the President on this one. We want to get to work."

As temperatures inched upward throughout the month of April Jake watched the snow piles shrink day by day. Walking to the Post Office at month end he saw that only the dirty snow mounds hiding on the shady side of the buildings still remained. Back at the bunkhouse he waved a small card at the fat cook.

"Got a post card from Oleg and Kosta. Looks like they're still in training at Camp Lewis."

The cook glared at him. "What the hell you talking about? Those boys can't write English."

"I know that. That's why I gave them a stack of postcards addressed to the bunkhouse before they left. Told them to drop one in the mail now and then so we'll be able to tell from the post mark where they are. This one is from Camp Lewis, Washington."

"Better than no news at all I guess."

By early May summer was in sight but Mac was concerned about Hans, for he knew that the big German's plans to make up his poker losses through more poker were rapidly depleting the hard-working man's money supply. "The railroad is hiring," said Mac to Jake. "I expect there will be more contract work when the snow melts up north, but you need to get Hans busy so he'll to stop gambling before he is completely broke."

"I know. Hans is learning the hard way that the poker table leans both ways, but the four of us want to keep the Damn Yankees together if we can."

"Just heard from Commissioner Edes," said Gerig to Mac at mid-month. "He'll be back in Alaska soon. And, he says that he expects Congress to continue funding this project."

"I'm sure as hell glad to hear that," said Mac.

"I am too," said Gerig. "Now if we can just get Congress to send some summer up here. The Susitna River is still too high to be navigable, the trails are still in bad shape and the snow north of Talkeetna is still too deep to get the station man crews back to work."

"It has been a difficult winter," said Mac. "There isn't much railroad being built." *And Hans lost everything playing poker!*

Anchorage War Garden

Chapter Thirty

"Summer is almost here," said Mr. Gerig to Mac on a brilliantly sunny late May morning. "The numbers are up, the geese are back, the woods are abloom and Commissioner Edes is on his way back to Alaska. I just got word that he plans to be back up here by early June."

When July rolled around without an Edes sighting Mac asked Mr. Gerig, "I thought Mr. Edes was going to be here by now?"

"Turns out he didn't get out of Seattle until the 18th of June, and when he got here he set off for Fairbanks and Nenana to inspect conditions on the north end of the railroad."

"Guess that explains why he's not been seen around here."

Crankiness was written all over Gerig's face when he said, "He and Mr. Mason, his personal secretary, made it to Fairbanks and they'll be on their way back soon. They're going to travel from Fairbanks to Chitina by automobile, ride the Copper River and Northwestern Railway from there to Cordova, and then sail on a United States lighthouse tender to Seward.

"Seems like an odd way to inspect our rail line," said Mac, "traveling along the route where we aren't."

Gerig nodded his head. "And when they finally get to Seward I have to take Mrs. Edes, Mrs. Mason and some other folks down to meet them. From there the expanded inspection party will travel to Anchorage, by steamship."

Mac said what he guessed Gerig was thinking. "Again avoiding the railroad they are inspecting."

The fat cook looked completely out of place standing in the middle of the engineer-designed nineteen-and-a-half-foot by seventy-foot garden with a hoe in his hand. A portion of the Anchorage town site was converted to garden plots so people could grow their own vegetables and throughout the summer of 1918 patriotic residents worked diligently to produce food in a land better known for producing glaciers and polar bears. The cook glared at Toot and said, "I am a chef, not a damn gardener."

"I was hoping you'd be better at gardening," said Toot, looking askance at the crooked rows of greenery. "And I ain't real fond of spending my Saturday's playing farmer either, but the railroad set up this victory garden because they want us to grow cabbage and other green shit, and by damn we're going to try."

The fat cook wiped the sweat from his thick neck and swatted at the mosquitoes in the same motion. "But this is Alaska. How the hell can we grow cabbage up here where the summer starts and ends in the same month?"

"Well these weeds are sure as hell growing good," Toot said as he returned to his hoeing. "Last summer folks learned that these twenty hour days, even in short number, produced big cabbage."

"Well yippety shit! What will I do with a garden full of cabbage?"

"Cook it. It'll be a change from those damn potatoes you've been serving us seven days a week: boiled potatoes, baked potatoes, potato bread, and that disgusting potato candy."

"Just trying to save some money, and help win the war."

"I'm tired of potatoes. We'll grow cabbage and make sauerkraut. It'll go well with those German concoctions you and Hans cook up."

"Shush. Don't be talking about that stuff. It ain't patriotic to be cooking German food with this war on."

"And it ain't patriotic to be German either," said Toot. "Guess that's why Hans is a Norwegian now."

The cook finally beamed. "And why the hell not. Gotta go along with the times you know. The government sure as hell did when they announced that sauerkraut is really a Dutch dish and said it's now okay for loyal Americans to eat the stuff again."

186

"The government also wants us to use other local produce when we can," said Toot. "The wild red currants are thick along the railroad up by Eklutna so the railroad is running a special train so folks can go pick them. You should go."

"Well I do have a delightful recipe for tenderloin of moose garnished with a fresh red currant sauce."

The sun was still high in the sky when Toot said to Mac after dinner one evening. "Let's mosey over to the post office and check the mail."

"Good idea, said Mac. *Give us a chance to walk off the cook's latest creation.*

The small post box popped open when Toot dialed the secret sequence of numbers. "Another postcard from Oleg and Kosta, with a post mark from France."

What's it say? asked Mac.

"Same as all the other cards. 'Greetings from wherever the postmark says.' Exactly what Jake wrote on the cards when he gave them to Oleg and Kosta."

The railroad presented its workers with a summer surprise by bumping the wage scale for unskilled laborers to fifty-five cents per hour, forty-seven percent more than they got just three years prior.

"You'll be getting a raise too," said Gerig to the Horse-riding-assistant-to-the-temporary-boss, "but you are going to earn it. I want that gap on the south end closed by the end of the month. The railroad camp at Rainbow will be your home until that line is open."

As he rode Lucky to the Rainbow camp Mac knew the Anchorage Division crews were busy working to the south while Seward Division crews worked northward, both determined to be the first to reach mile 79, the demarcation line between the two divisions. August was only four days old when Mac settled into the camp.

"You're off to a good start," he said to the rail gang foreman at days' end. "The gap is one thousand three hundred and fifty feet smaller than it was this morning."

Over the next few days Mac watched approvingly as crews rapidly finished the grading work, and track work followed close behind. Mac was able to report to Mr. Gerig that during the second week of August eleven thousand six hundred feet of rail was laid from Falls Creek to Indian Creek.

Mr. Gerig will like these numbers, thought Mac as he prepared his next weekly report showing the gap shrinking from both ends. But, Mac still feared that good news was chased by bad and the gathering rain clouds seem to validate his worries as he rode Lucky between the slowly converging rail lines. Though it was still August the cold rain and wind blowing off Cook Inlet soon turned to a deluge. Water poured off Mac's big hat, soaking through his heavy coat and chilling him to the bone. *The grading work will surely be delayed*, his head now told him.

Mac was pleased to see that the rail gang was still on the job despite the pounding rain, but he also saw that there was little activity. "Suppose this rain makes it hard to get much work done," he said to the dripping wet foreman.

"Hell no, we can handle the rain just fine. But we can't build a rail line when we don't have any rail, bolts and angle bars. I told the bean counters in Anchorage that we were running low, but now were flat out."

"Seems that bad news comes in batches," said Mac to the foreman. "Get these men inside where they can dry out and warm up, and I'll see if I can build a fire under the folks back in town."

How the hell will I ever meet Mr. Gerig's month-end completion goal, thought Mac as he waited for his phone call to be connected to the Supply Department in Anchorage. "Hello," he said when the Supply Clerk answered, and then asked, "Where in the hell are the materials I need to finish this rail line?"

Through the static Mac heard the sound of papers being shuffled before the clerk finally said, "Those parts are on their way from Seattle aboard the steamship *Anyox*."

"How the hell are we going to get this rail line built when you pencil-pushers keep working against us," Mac yelled in to the small cone shaped plastic receiver protruding from the front of the wooden telephone hanging on the wall. "And why are we only getting the material now, when we have known for months that we needed the rail this summer?"

When the supply clerk said, "Nigel's iron clad 'No Requisition, No Purchase Order' rule is the cause of the delay," Mac slammed the ear-piece on to the telephone's cradle.

"Rules are rules," Nigel explained matter-of-factly when Mac got a phone connection to the inept bureaucrat's gilded office.

"Nigel, you're as useless as the 'P' in ptarmigan!"

Despite the complacency of Nigel and crew, good fortune overcame bureaucracy when the rains ended and the grading work resumed. Track laying work was restarted on September 6th when the *Anyox* arrived with the needed materials. Rail was soon in place south to mile 81.4 and north to mile 77.25 leaving only a four-mile gap.

"The finish line is in sight," said Mac as he urged the weary crew onward.

Last Rail on Seward to Anchorage Line

H.G. Kaiser, Alaska Railroad Collection; Anchorage Museum,
B1979.002.AEC.G910

Chapter Thirty-one

On the afternoon of September 10th a small crowd gathered at mile 78.75 on the narrow ledge that had been arduously hewn from Alaska's ancient mountain to make way for Alaska's new rail line. As he watched the north and south lines being joined the chilly overcast weather reminded Mac that summer was already over.

"Be sure to let your workers know how grateful I am for all they did to get this job done," said Mac to the rail gang foreman. "We didn't make Mr. Gerig's end-of-August goal, but we beat the Seward gang to the finish line."

"We did, and now that the work is done the dignitaries take over," the foreman said as the elusive Commissioner Edes appeared to drive the final spike.

That evening Mac learned that the news had already been passed to Secretary Lane via telegraph, who quickly replied with:

"Chairman Edes and the Men of the Alaska Railway, I have just heard that the Alaskan road is completed between Matanuska and Seward. This is a matter of great gratification and begins a new day in the history of Alaska, which now will be able to reveal to the world more fully her resources, draw new people to the Territory, and become more perfectly an integral part of our Nation. Let me thank you, one and all, for your enthusiastic devotion to this work."

"Mighty thoughtful of Secretary Lane to remember us working folks," one weary rail gang worker said to Mac.

"Yeah, but he'll also distribute the message to newspapers throughout the country. Makes me wonder whose back he's patting."

Formal ceremonies marking the completion were held on September 29th and the railroad soon offered regular transportation service over the new line. The government railroad in Alaska now ran continuously from mile 0 at Seward to mile 209 at Montana Creek, with a thirty-eight-mile branch to the coal mines in the Matanuska Valley.

"Can't question our commitment to the war effort," said Mac, back at the bunkhouse table again. "This is the third time this week we've had cabbage soup for dinner."

"Shchi," the cook said under his breath.

"Ain't just our commitment to the war," said Toot, "Our grocery budget is pretty skinny these days. Our vacancy rate keeps climbing so we've had to do some belt tightening around here."

"So just how tight is our belt?" asked Mac.

"We're covering our fixed expenses and the cook still gets paid, but we've had to expand his duties again. He does a little gardening now too."

"And I had to go berry picking with a train load of women," the cook said as he refilled the soup bowls.

"That many women around here now?" asked Mac with feigned nonchalance.

"More all the time," said Toot. "As the men leave for the war more jobs are filled by women."

"In fact, I'm thinking about starting a gourmet night right here at the NEW Bunkhouse Royale," the fat cook said. "Braunschweiger, colcannon, moussaka, solyanka, lutefisk. Could raise some revenue you know."

"We could use the income," said Mac, "but we might want to let that idea stew just a bit longer."

You'd think I'm Mr. Gerig's Chair-Riding-Assistant, thought Mac, back at the Gee-Oh-Bee attending the endless stream of meetings that consume the days of office dwellers.

"The rail gang that just connected the south end line is preparing to move up to Montana Creek," said Gerig to the swarm in the stuffy overheated room. "As soon as the bridge is completed they'll push the line northward as far as possible before freeze up."

"But winter is breathing down our neck," said the construction superintendent, "and the rail and hardware isn't in Alaska yet."

Mac sat back and listened as Nigel tried in vain to justify the bureaucratic paralysis being inflicted on the project. *Funding, requisition, purchase order, shipment and then delivery,* Mac thought. *Everything has to be in sequence but whoever established the pecking order forgot to add old man winter in to the equation.*

"Nigel, you're telling us the damn paperwork is more important than railroad building," said an exasperated looking Gerig. "Are you for us or against us?"

The question went unanswered, but the discussion dragged on. Mac kept one ear on the conversation but his mind wandered as he gazed out at the twin steel rails running through the Anchorage yard, the same rails as before, yet very different. The continuous line now stitched together a significant swath of Alaska he realized, smiling now as the gravity of the accomplishment took seat. *This railroad is going to be different from the others up here in Alaska. The government, on their own damn schedule, is going to see this project through to the end. Seward and Fairbanks will be forever tied together and Anchorage will be the heart of that line.*

When the meeting finally ended late in the afternoon Gerig pulled Mac aside and said, "There is one more thing I'd like you to do today Mac. We just moved a group of women into the cottage where Mr. Mears used to live and I'd like you to stop by there on your way home and make sure they have everything they need."

Warm light glowing through the windows greeted Mac as he gingerly stepped on to the large front porch of the sturdy house on the bluff above the rail yard. He had fearlessly conquered the many challenges of Alaskan living but he was absolutely aquiver as he knocked on the door to check on the wellbeing of the female Alaskans.

The woman opening the door took Mac by surprise, younger and prettier than he'd dared to imagine. "Evening ma'am," said Mac tentatively and politely, hat in hand, as the slender yet not skinny woman opened the front door. "I'm Mac. Mr. Gerig asked me to stop by and make sure everything is okay with the house." Their eyes met briefly before Mac nervously looked away, as if checking the house.

"I'm Prudence," the young lady said with a warm smile. "The house is just fine." She stepped back and opened the door wider. "Let me take your hat and coat, if you can join us for a moment." Mac remained ill at ease, his experience with women being largely limited to the type that follow mining camps full of young men with new found wealth, but he cautiously followed the svelte young woman into the living room.

"These are my housemates," she said as she introduced him to three women who worked at the Telegraph and Telephone office and one who worked in the Commission's Accounting office. Miss Prudence and one other were teachers in the Anchorage Public Schools.

The parlor was homey. *Like the bunkhouse parlor, but in an opposite sort of way.* The satisfying flowery smells a contrast to the familiar stale smoke smell of the bunkhouse. The eye-catching bright coverlets carefully placed on the furniture unlike the dark manly seating he was accustomed to. The pleasant tidiness contrary to the lived-in feeling of the man camp.

Mac soon found himself enjoying the feminine company, as well as the mouth-watering smells from the smokeless kitchen. "What persuaded you ladies to come up here to Alaska?" he asked.

"Adventure," said one of the women.

When another said, "A chance to see Alaska before we settle down," Mac understood that Alaska and settling down were separate components of their life plans.

Prudence excused herself to go to the kitchen and as she returned asked, "Won't you join us for dinner?"

"I'd be pleased to," he said, surprised at the ease with which he accepted. During the tasty meatless meal the young women asked him many questions about his years in Alaska and seemed genuinely interested in the stories he shared.

When the beaming Mac returned to the bunkhouse later that evening Toot asked, "You been at the gin joint again?"

"Nope," said Mac, leaving the smile unexplained.

The bridge over Montana Creek was completed in early September but October was on the calendar before the rail and fittings arrived in Anchorage, finally allowing the rail gang to begin installing rail north from the new bridge. When the track laying machine was assembled on October 21st the temperature was one degree below zero. The steel gang began laying track the following day, but the fast approaching winter soon ended their work for the year.

The news was flashed around the world and up to Alaska when the war in Europe ended on November 11th.

"Oleg and Kosta will be on their way home soon," said Jake to the celebrative crowd at the bunkhouse.

Mac shared in the jubilation, but his ever alert gut instinct refused to allow him to accept that all was now good in the world.

The men checked the post office frequently, awaiting another postcard, hopefully from New York or Seattle, but none came. Finally, long after the war was over they received a letter from France, but it was from their friends' platoon sergeant.

Mac's face told the story even before he informed his friends that in the waning days of the great war Oleg and Kosta had died fighting for their adopted country.

"They were killed in a gas attack," said Mac to the grief-stricken group as he read the letter. "Apparently they didn't understand the warnings and failed to don their gas masks in time."

The bunkhouse was still in mourning when the Spanish flu pandemic that was sweeping the globe made its way to Alaska, proving Mac's theory that while good news is a loner, bad news travels in packs. Anchorage schools were closed and dances, lodge meetings and church services were forbidden, but the influenza still spread through the town and then moved on to the construction camps along the rail line. A large warehouse in Talkeetna was converted to a hospital to care for workers as well as local natives. In an attempt to keep the disease from spreading to Interior Alaska guards were placed on the Broad Pass trail to prevent anyone from traveling up to Nenana.

As the winter solstice marked the shortest day of what had been a long year for William Gerig he asked Mac to join him in his office.

"We didn't get much done this year, Mac." Gerig spoke in a tone reeking of frustration. "With the war and all our average monthly work force was only two thousand five hundred and fifty compared to four thousand four hundred and sixty-six last year."

"We do have a continuous rail line from Seward that is moving north," said Mac, "toward the line that's moving south from Nenana. And there is now a winter trail connecting the two."

"The lack of progress is disappointing," said Gerig, "but the human losses are heartbreaking."

Mac was surprised as he watched the man who seldom bared his soul let the burdens he was carrying rise to the surface.

"The pervasive tragedies of the war and the flu epidemic get me down, but it's the preventable personal tragedies that break my spirit. Like when Allenbaugh fell under a moving locomotive, and when Steinman was run over by a box car."

As Gerig's eyes welled up Mac swallowed and looked out the window to spare the man's dignity. He turned his own watery eyes back when Gerig said, "The worst day of this year was when the launch sank in the muddy waters of the Tanana River, drowning the wife of the Resident Engineer in Fairbanks along with seven others."

Probably wishes he was back in Panama, thought Mac.

The men's thoughts remained private for several moments as they regained their composure, then Gerig said, "We just have to buck up and take it, because we're learning that operating a railroad in Alaska is just as difficult as building a railroad in Alaska. The snow has now blocked the Anchorage to Seward line, forcing passengers and freight to be transferred around snow slides."

"We'll just have to work harder next year," said Mac, trying to end the discussion on a positive note.

Gerig's face remained strained. "We will, but there is only so much we can do without money, and the Commission is broke again."

General Office Building

H.G. Kaiser, Alaska Railroad Collection; Anchorage Museum,
B1979.002.AEC.G1917

Chapter Thirty-two

The always dark and disquieting month of January was particularly worrisome in 1919, the year whose last name echoed its first. The germinal momentum that had pushed the railroad far into Alaska and spawned the city of Anchorage was now ebbing. The Interior Secretary had conceded that due to increasing labor, material and transportation costs the original thirty-five-million-dollar budget would not be adequate to complete the project. There was much left to be done but only four million dollars remained unspent, and uncertainties on when the money would be available now threatened to bring work to a halt.

Nigel, the accountant who thought himself the boss looked up from the ledger lying on his table when Mac and Mr. Gerig, the real boss, came into his office unannounced.

"Seems like they want this railroad built," said Gerig, "but they won't give us the damn money when we need it."

Nigel LeCount listened attentively as Gerig paced back and forth across the den of accountancy.

"There is good reason for the government to operate on a fiscal year," said Nigel, but failed to define the reason.

"That's a load of manure," said Mac. "Truth is you've lived with this wrongheaded cycle for so long that you think July 1st is New Year's Day."

As Nigel again attempted to justify the unjustifiable Gerig silenced him with a stern look. "Must have taken a pile of Washington wisdom to get your sacred accounting cycle exactly backwards."

With a conciliatory look on his typically indifferent face LeCount said, "Mr. Mears warned them about that back in 1915."

"Obviously no one listened," said Gerig. "Washington continues to dole out money according to political whims and bureaucratic schedules."

"Funding for this project has always been disjointed," said Mac.

Gerig stopped pacing and glared at Nigel. "Now here we are in a financial bind again. We have people out working and we don't know how much longer we can pay them. The crew just completed the rail line to Talkeetna and the bridge over the Talkeetna River is under construction, but we can't expect those crews to keep working if can't pay them."

"At least we've been able to generate more revenue now that the line to Seward is open," said Nigel. "That will help meet some of the payroll."

"How the hell can we be making money on that route, with the damn snow slides blocking the rail line," said Gerig as he prepared to leave.

In early February Mac reported to the bunkhouse forum that Secretary Lane had requested over thirteen million dollars from Congress to fund continuing construction and asked them to pass the appropriation before the session ended in early March.

"I'll get the community behind this," said Jake, and the Anchorage Chamber of Commerce swiftly endorsed the request in a cable to Commissioner Edes, who was once again back in Washington. But, Washington wasn't listening. Congress adjourned on March 4th without passing the appropriation and President Wilson sailed from New York on March 5th for a peace conference in Paris.

The next day Mac and Gerig were back in Nigel's office.

"If Washington tried to build a railroad it would have three rails," said Gerig angrily. "I just issued a statement saying that even though no definite plans have been made to deal with the lack of funding, arrangements can be made to maintain the present staffing. I expect you, LeCount, to make those arrangements!"

"You know that regulations do not allow us to spend money that we do not have," said Nigel LeCount.

The chair fell backwards and crashed to the floor as Gerig stood in a rush. "I'll be damned if I'm going fire the workers we need to build this railroad, simply because the elected morons in Washington can't make a damn decision!" He was leaning over LeCount's desk now, boss-like again.

Nigel maintained his stoic look and pronounced. "But the rules say..."

"Damn the rules! You tradition bound bureaucrats assume that if you always do things the same way you must be right."

Nigel stiffened now. "But the rules..."

"Or, you'll occasionally do something that is politically appropriate and not care if it's right or wrong."

Nigel tilted his head and tried again. "But the..."

"For once we are going to do something simply because it is the right goddamn thing to do."

Nigel, with a humble look on his face now. "But..."

"LeCount, you can either find a way to keep our work force in place until this dysfunctional damn government gets their shit together or I will find someone who can."

A classic conundrum, thought Mac. *Washington won't provide money to pay the railroad workers, Mr. Gerig won't lay them off, and Nigel has to find a solution.*

The light in Nigel's house of numbers burned late as he sat beneath his favorite green eyeshade searching for a rule that would allow him to break the rules.

When Mac strode in early the next morning, anxious to learn how the dilemma would be resolved, Nigel was waiting outside the bosses' office. Mac and the bleary-eyed number cruncher sat silently, waiting for Gerig to arrive.

When Gerig marched in and simply said, "Morning," to Nigel, the tone of the single word greeting told Mac that omission of the word good was not an oversight.

"Good day," said Nigel, hopefully, as Gerig led them into his office.

"So, explain our plan to keep this organization intact while we wait for Congress to get off their dead ass and do something."

"Well, we can't spend money that hasn't been appropriated, nor can we expect people to work without pay, but there is a third option. We can ask them to work at a reduced pay, and make up the difference when the next appropriation comes through."

"But we don't know when that will be."

"We certainly cannot be sure, but my contacts in Washington tell me the President will call the Congress back in session before June."

"Congress, the same dunderheads who failed to pass an appropriation before they adjourned."

"Yes, but..."

"Okay! We'll ask people to work for partial pay," said Gerig, ending the discussion. "An imperfect solution, but these are imperfect times."

Mears' Residence

Angier Family Papers,
UAF-1969-89-94, Archives, University of Alaska Fairbanks

Chapter Thirty-three

Word that railroaders would be paid only about twenty-five percent of their earnings spread across the property before the official announcement got out of the Gee-Oh-Bee. The workers were not happy but most stayed on the job.

"It ain't that they trust the government," said Toot to Mac that evening. "It's that they ain't got any other jobs to go to."

"We're lucky to have them," said Mac. "But the railroad is hunkering down trying to survive just when we should be gearing up for the construction season."

"The crews are still on the job," said Toot, "gambling that Congress will eventually come through with the money. Instead of greenbacks they're getting IOUs."

"True enough," said Mac, "not unlike those match sticks the Damn Yankees use."

Toot lit up at that. "Yeah, the same government that won't allow gambling in this town is saying, 'you can bet on us, we might pay you some day.'"

"This is why it's good for this railroad to have our own revenue," said Mac, "But we spend too much money to produce that income."

"So our outgo is more than our income," said Toot.

"You're absolutely right. The real question will be whether we can generate revenue faster than we generate expenses."

April was on the calendar when Mac came home and tossed the latest edition of the *Anchorage Daily Times* on the kitchen table. "The bastards will never let up on us. Now they've printed a letter from some group in Seward calling itself the Alaska Association. The *Times* calls their attack on us ill-begotten, but they still printed the bullshit letter."

The cook looked up from the big pot he was stirring on the stove and wiped his hands on his apron. "What the hell is this so-called association?" he asked, coming over to look at the paper.

"I'm sure it's bogus," said Mac. "No doubt that rotten bastard Ballaine is behind it. There isn't much that phony son-of-a-bitch won't do to get even with this railroad."

"Sounds to me like he's getting his information from someone inside the railroad," said Jake as he read through the offensive letter.

"That's exactly what I suspect," Mac spit out, "but I wonder who the hell it is?"

Toot answered that one. "I'm guessing that culprit's initials would be N-I-G-E-L. That scheming bastard even looks like a cross between a weasel and a stool pigeon. My B & B gang has been busy remodeling the space that was used by the Railroad YMCA and that little rat bastard is always lurking about."

Mac sat at the table. "I thought the Railroad Men's Club was taking over that space?"

"They are. We're just getting it fancied up for them. It'd be a good place for you to take that little teacher on a date."

"You just tend to your own business," said Mac. But, the young woman had been on his mind all winter. *When I see her around town her smile is warm and friendly. Maybe Toot is right. Maybe she would be willing to go on a date with me.*

Prudence answered the door when Mac stopped by the rented home one sunny but chilly evening and the warmth of her greeting said she was clearly pleased to see the tall man.

"Just stopped by to make sure everything is okay," said Mac timidly, "with the house."

"The house is fine, Mac. How are you?"

"Just fine, ma'am, just fine," he said quickly, gaining confidence. "Sure is nice to see the longer days."

"Indeed it is, but I really didn't find the winter as horrible as folks said it would be."

"Alaskan winters are just fine," said Mac," If you get out and do things."

"I certainly agree with you. My housemates tell me the newest thing is the remodeled Railroad Men's Club, but I've not been there yet."

"Well, if you might be willing to go with me this Saturday evening I'd be pleased to show you around. We could even try out the bowling lanes if you'd like?"

"Why I'd love that, Mac."

After yet another appropriation measure failed to pass both houses of Congress, the Commission put out notices discouraging people from seeking employment with the railroad. There would be no new hires but the existing workforce was still on the job.

On July 1st fiscal year 1919 - 1920 rolled in with two million dollars for the Commission and within days railroaders started receiving their back pay. In one week one hundred and seventy-three thousand dollars were distributed to employees in the Anchorage Division and disbursing agents traveled to outlying areas to distribute money owed to workers.

With newfound pay burning a hole in his pocket Toot stopped by the Men's Club to treat himself to a candy bar. When he saw Poetic Pete he said with a sly look, "I hear my friend Mac is getting so serious about bowling that he's given up whiskey."

Pete replied with.

> The Bunkhouse boys were whooping it up,
> at an edge-of-town saloon.
> While in Anchor town the tall man sulked,
> and walked the streets alone.
> He longed for a house and a beautiful wife,
> and the happiness they'd bring.
> But good women were scarce as an outhouse breeze,
> in a land always longing for spring.

He seemed destined to remain a solitary man,
then he met that special gal.
He takes her bowling and she makes him smile;
she's freed him from his lonely hell.
Enraptured by his Alaskan Madonna,
he bid his lonely life adieu.
She's his constant companion, his light-o-love,
the lady that's known as Pru.

Engine No. 265 at Eska

Alaska State Library, Alaska Purchase Centennial Collection,
P.S. Hunt, ASL-P20-179

Chapter Thirty-four

Upon returning from France in May of 1919 Colonel Frederick Mears went to the Alaska Engineering Commission office in Washington, D.C. and immediately began helping prepare a funding request for continuation of the railroad in Alaska. By July the new budget was ready, projecting a total cost that went from thirty-five million dollars up to fifty-two million.

Mears knew the future of the railroad was on the line when the House Committee on Territories announced that four days of hearings would be held on a bill to amend the original 1914 legislation by adding the additional seventeen million dollars needed to complete the project, and changing the completion date to December 31, 1922. The changes would cover delays and cost increases attributed to the war.

DAY ONE – Mears was paying close attention when the hearings opened at 11:00 a.m. on Wednesday, July 23rd under the direction of the Honorable Charles F. Curry of California.

The Assistant Secretary of the Interior reported that 366 miles of mainline rail and branches were in operation and that the project was about two-thirds complete, with a gap in the midsection of the line and a thirty-four-mile gap between Nenana and Fairbanks. He also reported that while they planned to have the rail line completed by the end of 1921 the bridge over the Tanana River near Nenana would not be ready until the end of 1922.

Commission engineer J.L. McPherson presented detailed estimates on the work needed to complete the project and the cost of each component. In addition to the rail line yet to be completed, there were five major bridges to be built. The request also covered estimated operating losses through December 31, 1921, anticipating that the railroad would incur over four dollars in expenses for each dollar of income they generated.

The Committee adjourned for the day after being in session for seventy-five minutes.

DAY TWO -- The Committee was back at work at 11:00 a.m. sharp on Thursday. Commission engineer McPherson completed his presentation and then responded to a wide variety of Committee questions about the cost of the Commission's weekly newspaper, freight rates and town site development. The audience listened patiently as the elected representatives of the people asked questions about reindeer, cattle and caribou.

Mr. Strong, Representative from Kansas. "What kind of meat does the reindeer make?"

Mr. McPherson. "The reindeer is very similar to venison; if anything, it is sweeter."

Mr. Monahan, Representative from Wisconsin. "In the raising of reindeer herds and musk ox herds are there wolves or other destroying agencies there?"

Mr. McPherson. "Yes."

Mr. Dowell, Representative from Iowa. "What can the cattle live on up there?"

Mr. McPherson. "The grass."

Mr. Monahan. "Are there many caribou in that country?"

Mr. McPherson. "They are probably numbered by the hundreds of thousands."

Chairman Curry. "The caribou is a wild animal, is it not?"

Mr. McPherson. "The caribou has never been a domesticated animal."

The Committee returned to more relevant issues when Representative Brooks from Pennsylvania said, "I know that to pay the expenses of operating that road will require the hauling of a great deal of freight, and the estimate of $52,000,000 will require the hauling of a good deal of freight to pay the interest on that. Of course, we don't expect to get revenue enough to pay the running expenses, operation of the road, and interest too, for some time."

Mr. McPherson agreed. "I do not anticipate that revenues from freight and passenger operations traffic will pay for operation and maintenance expenses for a number of years; but with the development of the resources tributary to this line, there is no question in my mind that ultimately the traffic will pay and pay well."

DAY THREE – The Committee was back on the job at the crack of eleven on Friday morning, the 25th of July. Albert Johnson, representative from the state of Washington spoke in favor of funding the completion of the line, but also said that, "I have come to the conclusion that the three commissioners sent to Alaska to build the railroad did not realize the magnitude of the project and did not act in harmony." But, he added that, "Now we must go ahead and we will have to pass this measure. I think it would be a good proposition if this committee could secure the assurance somewhere along the line that a little different plan of business management will be undertaken in the future building of the railroad."

Upon completion of Mr. Johnson's testimony, the Committee adjourned, with plans to reconvene six days later.

DAY FOUR – When the Committee reconvened at 10:30 a.m. on the following Thursday the Chairman inserted in the record articles from several newspapers supporting the additional money, and then a statement was made by Commissioner Edes.

Edes, who had been seriously ill and had not attended the prior sessions, recapped the history of the project and the Alaska Engineering Commission. Edes also fielded numerous questions about his role on the Commission and in particular his numerous absences from Alaska. He defended his actions, pointing out that he was in Alaska during the construction season and in Washington, D.C. during the winter months to assure that Congress provided the funding needed for the following season. He also noted that there were competent managers in charge in Alaska at all times and that he was in contact with them during his absences.

Finally, Colonel Mears made a statement and then again described the problems created by the sporadic funding of the project.

Prior to adjournment, the Committee voted unanimously to report the bill with a favorable recommendation to be made by the chairman. As he left the room Mears realized that the project's future, though not yet secure, was brighter.

Halloway Party at Deadhorse Hill

H.G. Kaiser, Alaska Railroad Collection; Anchorage Museum,
B1979.002.AEC.G1451

Chapter Thirty-five

"So our new boss is the old boss; or is our old boss the new boss?" Toot asked as he and Mac ambled along Ship Creek on a sunny summer evening.

Mac watched the spawning salmon rushing upstream to end their days with the same enthusiasm they'd showed when exiting the stream at the dawn of their days. "Yes, Mr. Mears is on his way back. The Interior Secretary named him Chairman and Chief Engineer of the Alaska Engineering Commission. Edes resigned from the Commission because of his poor health, but now he's a Consulting Engineer for the project."

"What is going to happen to our temporary boss?" asked Toot, "and to you?"

"Gerig will still be the engineer in charge of the Anchorage Division, and I'll be Mr. Mears' assistant again."

"Mears will get this project moving. Ain't no moss growing under that man's ass."

"I know," said Mac. "He and his family are already on their way to Alaska."

There was a hint of fall in the air as Mac walked along the rectangular Anchorage streets under a blue mid-August sky. The green leaves were a bit less vibrant, the wild flowers were fading, the smell of summer's growth was gone and the smell of fall's decay was just around the bend. But, in the season of decline Mac's spirits were on the rise.

When Mac checked in with his boss Gerig immediately said, "Colonel Mears and his party will arrive in Seward on August 21st. I'll be taking a special train to pick them up on the 22nd and they want to head north as soon as possible. I need you to arrange a first rate tour for them. These aren't our typical rubberneckers Mac; these are important folks. Take good care of them."

"Anything special they want to see?"

"They'll want to inspect all rail operations and construction activity between here and Fairbanks. And we want them to see it all, the working line up to the coal mines, the unfinished gaps up north, the unbridged rivers, even the mistakes we made last winter."

"So we'll be traveling by train and horseback."

"That's right," said Gerig. "You can take the train up to the end of the line, but you'll need to travel on horseback through the gap to catch the rail line again south of Nenana."

"How big of a party is this going to be?" asked Mac.

"Mears and his five guests for sure. There are senior executives from three major railroad companies, Assistant Interior Secretary Hallowell and the head of the U.S. Geological Survey, Dr. Brooks. Sounds like some of the wives will go along too, at least part of the way. Mr. Mears wants to show them Alaska as well as the rail project so you'll be doing some sightseeing too, maybe even some hunting and fishing."

"I'll have things all arranged," said Mac. "We'll take whatever we need to make them comfortable."

Mac enthusiastically began assembling the tents and other gear they would need for an extended trip into wild Alaska. Menus were prepared and arrangements were made to have horses waiting up at the end of steel. *I'll finally be the Horse-Riding-Assistant to Mr. Mears again*, thought Mac, happily.

The bunkhouse bath was busy that Saturday afternoon as both Mac and Toot spruced up to attend the public reception for Mears and the visiting officials at the Anchorage Chamber of Commerce room in the Empress Theater.

"Yer a respectable looking fella when you get all cleaned up and put yer church clothes on," said Toot to Mac as the squeaky clean duo waited in the bunkhouse parlor.

"You look mighty respectable in church clothes yourself," said Mac.

Toot looked at his reflection in the window, carefully touching up his slicked back red hair and brushing the lapels on his jacket. "I'm attending this shindig cuz Jake is out of town and asked me to be the Chamber representative from the NEW Bunkhouse Royale. I suppose yer going so you have an excuse to take that school teacher somewhere fancy."

"Just anxious to welcome Mr. Mears and his family back in Alaska."

"I'd like to introduce you to my friend Prudence," said Mac to Mr. and Mrs. Mears when they finally got close to the honored guests. Anchorage was out in force and Mac was proud to be escorting Miss Prudence, with rosy cheeks that complemented her hazel eyes. The practical yet pretty dress she wore was overshadowed by her bright smile.

As Prudence and Jane Mears discussed their mutual interest in the education of Anchorage's children the two men renewed their friendship. Mac reported on the happenings in Alaska and then said, "I'm told you increased the efficiency of the rail operation in France."

"We did, largely because that project didn't require long waits for federal appropriations."

"And now you're back here playing the waiting game again," said Mac as he and Prudence moved on to allow others to greet the honored guests.

"A very nice couple," said Prudence to Mac as they moved to their designated seats. "She is obviously very passionate about education."

"They both get things done. Mrs. Mears was a driving force behind establishment of a good school here in Anchorage. And of course the Colonel is the one who got the railroad project going. And, though he'll never mention it, he received the Grand Cross of the French Legion of Honor from the commander of the French Army, and the Distinguished Service Medal from General Pershing."

As they listened to local dignitaries speak optimistically about the future of Anchorage and the area along the new rail line Prudence reached under the table and found Mac's strong hand. With fingers entwined they listened to the assembled Alaskans tout the development they were already seeing along the rail corridor.

The next day Mac was back in his working clothes, the trademark cowboy hat atop his head, ready to head north with Mears and his guests. At the depot he tipped his hat to the assembled group of citified looking men and women. "We'll be traveling by train and then by horseback before the day is over."

As the long day ended the comfortable cots and warm bedding were laid out in the sturdy canvas tents and fresh-caught fish were cooking over an open fire. As the party sat around the campfire in the rapidly cooling evening air Mac entertained by telling Alaskan tales to attentive visitors from the east. "They called him Moose Liver Johnson..." he began.

For the next few days Mac watched the distinguished visitors absorbing the harsh, yet rich and spectacularly stunning land surrounding them; the many beautiful mountain views, the pungent yet pleasing smells of autumn and the sounds of the wind hurrying through the trees and water rushing over rocky stream beds. Mac tended the horses and kept the camp ready as the guests picked berries and caught fish and hunted caribou. Each evening when the chilled air stilled the pesky mosquitoes they gathered around the campfire.

"I can see why you love this north country," said Mrs. Hallowell to Mac on their last evening in camp.

Mac looked up with a smile as wide as the big valley. "Reckon that is why I agree with Robert Service when he says, '...there's some as would trade it for no land on earth — and I'm one.'"

The next morning as they broke camp and loaded their gear on the pack horses Mrs. Hallowell gave Mac a polite hug. "Thank you so much for sharing your Alaska with us. I've read that the Alaskan scenery will spoil those who do not stay, since nothing else can compare, and I now believe it."

Mr. Gerig escorted the other guests back to Anchorage while Mac accompanied Mears, Hallowell and Brooks as they turned their full attention to inspection of the railroad, moving on horseback to Hurricane Gulch.

"We'll have to build a four-hundred-foot long steel bridge to cross the deep chasm," said Mears. "We plan to build the steel bridges from south to north, so we can use the rail line to move the steel up to the work sites."

From Hurricane the inspection party climbed into the tundra, following the trail up to Broad Pass and on through the wide scenic valley.

"We are at the highest point on the rail line here, twenty-three hundred and forty-six feet above sea level," Mears pointed out as the group reached Summit Lake.

"This is a watershed divide," said Dr. Brooks. "Water flowing south from here ends up in Cook Inlet while water flowing north empties into the Yukon River and the Bering Sea. I've had the good fortune to make twenty-one trips to Alaska, mostly studying and mapping the arctic mountains north of the Yukon basin, and the land is as awe inspiring as it was when I first set eyes on it in 1904."

The valley narrowed as they moved on north, following the wagon road along the north-flowing Jack and then Nenana Rivers. They traveled single-file now, with Mears and his quests in front and Mac and the pack horses strung out behind.

"We'll have to build another high steel bridge here," said Mears as they stood on the edge of the ravine that carried Riley Creek down to the Nenana River.

A few miles further on they came to the narrow trail cut through the unstable soil on the steep walls of the ravine carved by the Nenana River. "Keep a tight rein here," said Mac. "If you go over the edge there will be nothing to stop you until you land in the icy water of the river below."

"The walls of this canyon are a dirt engineer's nightmare," said Mears. "Grading will be difficult and costly and we'll have to construct several wooden bridges and trestles, as well as tunnels." As they came out the north end of the canyon they joined up with the rail line again and followed the Nenana through the wide valley leading to the confluence of the Nenana and Tanana rivers.

Near the town of Nenana, the men inspected the remnants of the railroad's failed effort to build a timber pile bridge.

"During the winter of 1918-1919 we built tracks and trestles across frozen wetlands in order to get the rail line open to the coal mines south of Nenana," said Mac. "But not long after the first loads of coal were delivered to Fairbanks the spring thaw destroyed most of the winter's work."

"The work was done for the right reasons," said Mears, "as they needed the coal up in Fairbanks. And, we learned that we need to develop new techniques for building a railroad across permafrost."

A mile upstream Mears pointed out the site where a long steel bridge would ultimately cross the Tanana and link to the rail line running on to Fairbanks.

"The crossing here will be the largest bridge on the rail line," Mears said to the men, "and it will be the final link in the system."

"It's been a pleasure to show what's been accomplished up here," said Mears to Hallowell and Brooks as the two visitors prepared to continue on to Fairbanks and then down to Cordova. "Mac and I will head back to Anchorage and prepare to get this project wrapped up. The rail line is nearing completion, the bridges are being designed, and the workers are ready. All we need is the money."

"I'm confident the legislation will be approved soon," said Hallowell as he shook hands with Mears.

That prediction came true on October 7th when the railroad's funding bill became law.

Seventeen inches of snow had fallen on Anchorage on the day after Christmas and the cleanup was still in progress when Mac and Mears moved through the rail yard checking on the snow clearing work. Crews were busy plowing and shoveling the snow away from the tracks and roadways so rail operations could return to normal as quickly as possible.

"This white stuff is a part of every Alaskan winter," said Mac to Colonel Mears, so dealing with the snow will be part of the job for those who operate this railroad." As they watched the crews pushing the new snow in piles that would grow throughout the winter months Mac asked, "Will you stay on to run this organization after the construction is done?"

"I don't really know. What about you, Mac? You've been in Alaska a long time. You should stay on and help run this railroad."

"I hope to, sir. Anchorage is my home now."

"I'll do what I can to find a permanent job for you, Mac, but the first thing we have to do is get the rail line finished. We certainly didn't make much progress this year."

"This hasn't been a good construction year," said Mac. "The northbound track was extended only eleven miles, but track is now in place south from Nenana down to the foot of the Nenana canyon and a narrow gauge line now connects north Nenana with Fairbanks. The ends of steel on the main line are one hundred and twenty-two miles apart." Then, with the newfound optimism that he was still getting used to, Mac said, "but with you back and money in the bank next year will be much better."

PART FIVE
Completing the Project
(1920 through 1923)

Rotary Plow Cutting Through Slide

Frederick C. Mears Papers,
UAF-1984-75-84, Archives, University of Alaska Fairbanks

Chapter Thirty-six

Nineteen-twenty was supposed to be a good year, but the heavy snow that had fallen in December was soon buried deep beneath the snows of January, and the accumulating layers were once again wreaking havoc on the fledgling rail line. Now, the boss and his wife had been caught in a snow slide along the line south of town and the business car, designated the A-1, was deposited wheels up a few feet down the embankment.

"Are you okay, sir?" Mac asked Mears when the Colonel returned to Anchorage.

"We're just fine," said Mears. "The car held up well."

"I'm certainly glad that you and Mrs. Mears weren't hurt," said Mac. Then, the obvious, "Looks like we're in for a rough winter."

"We've learned how to build a railroad in Alaska," said Mears, "but we still have some things to learn about operating a railroad in Alaska. The snow shed we built over the track in the slide zone at mile 75 works well, but there was a large slide four miles south of the new shed and now this one that knocked my car right off the track."

Mac's solution was quick in coming. "Looks like we need to build more snow sheds."

"This is a country of extremes," said Mears, "that will require some extra precautions. The line between here and Seward passes through areas of high snow fall surrounded by steep mountains where the snow accumulates until it breaks loose and comes thundering down on our railroad."

"I know" said Mac, with the certainty of one who'd seen it all before.

Mears said nothing at first, then, "You know this country better than most folks, Mac. That's why I need you to take a close look at the line between here and Seward and tell me where you think the slides are most likely to hit us. The more we know about where the problems are developing the better we can deal with them."

The trip south reminded Mac that the rail line between Anchorage and Seward runs through an exceptionally scenic part of a land known for stunning scenery. Along the fjord-like Turnagain Arm he was entranced by the unending motion of the water trapped between two intimidating mountain ridges. Floating ice drifted in the tidal currents this time of year, but the always-moving seawater never froze solid. Mac noted the obvious slide zones along the steep snow-covered mountain slopes, natural ravines running from high on the mountain that became snow-filled chutes each winter.

At the head of the inlet they began the long climb up along the Placer River. The rail line was well back from the mountains framing the wide valley, and although the snow was deep there was little threat from slides.

Further south Mac looked up at heavy layers of new snow being added to the upper reaches of Spencer and Bartlett Glaciers. He knew the falling snow would pack into the immense slow moving ice rivers and begin its long journey down to the valley.

The frozen white surface of Upper and Lower Trail Lakes passed slowly by, and as the train rolled along Kenai Lake Mac wondered if the water sealed below the frozen white surface retained the turquoise-hued color that it displayed in summer.

Dropping through snow-covered forest land to Seward at the head of Resurrection Bay Mac realized, *I am indeed blessed. I'll likely never gaze upon the works of the great artists or visit the architectural wonders of the world, but I live in Mother Nature's gallery.*

Mac spent several days working with Seward-based maintenance and train crews to catalog the winter hazards that plagued the south end of the line, and learning about Seward's infamous John Ballaine.

"The man is committed to promoting Seward, and himself," one of the locals told Mac, "but he ain't always ethical. They claim he gets much of his information from a friend at the railroad."

On the morning of February 7th, Mac was headed home from Seward on the 8:00 a.m. train, certain that the double-header plow and flangers in front of the locomotive would get him and the other ninety passengers back to Anchorage by evening. His confidence faded as the train struggled through increasingly deep snow while climbing out of Seward. When the heavy snow brought the train to a halt just twelve miles out of town Mac asked the conductor, "What can I do to help?"

"Hang on tight, we're going to back down the grade to Seward."

As the train edged caboosewards toward Seward Mac saw that in the forty-five minutes that had elapsed since their uphill trek another eight inches had fallen on the track. After pushing through four miles of snow-covered railway the train stalled, unable to move in either direction.

"Get as many passengers to help as you can," the conductor said to Mac, "and come on out and help us clear snow."

"We're going to shovel our way out of here?" asked Mac.

"Afraid so. The snow plow that was the head end of this smoke-belching monster is now the tail, and it ain't doing any good back there."

Muscle power took over from the machine as Mac and the others cleared deep snow away from the tracks so the train could back slowly down the hill. As they worked Mac warned the helpful passengers of the many hazards of working outdoors in the Alaskan winter. "The slippery ice and snow will put you on the ground in an instant, and you'll hit like a ton of bricks. Keep your hands covered so your fingers don't freeze. Watch the people around you for signs of frostbite. And, enjoy the fresh air."

I won't be getting much rest tonight, Mac accepted on arrival back in Seward, as he was told to report to the depot that evening ready to go to work. Through the snowy night he worked alongside other railroaders, including extra gang crews and even the cook house employees. Together they fought the onslaught of snow until one by one exhaustion and icy cold feet and hands forced them back inside to warm up and rest. The snow still fell.

"All aboard," the conductor called the following morning as the train again departed for Anchorage.

"Are we going to make it today?" Mac asked the conductor, looking up at the reconfigured train. He saw that there was now a rotary plow, plus two locomotives, a passenger coach and baggage car.

The conductor flashed a confident look. "We're sure as hell going to try. With that big plow up front it'll take a ton of snow to stop us."

When we're moving forward, thought Mac.

Mac's watch said it was high noon when the heavy train rocked and rattled to a halt. Instinctively, he knew that the train was derailed before he asked the conductor, "need any help?"

"Sure do," was the reply from the weary man. "We have one car and one locomotive on the ground."

For the next three hours Mac worked alongside the other railroad workers as they cleared ice and packed snow away from the track and steel wheels. Mac stepped back and watched as the train crew carefully placed the steel ramp-like device called a rerailer in front of each off-rail wheel. He held his breath as locomotive power was gradually applied until the wheel slowly rolled back up on to the rail.

"We're ready to roll," the conductor said to Mac as the train got underway again, plowing through four-foot snow piles as they climbed up to the mile 45 summit. Mac's euphoria was short-lived for the train was soon delayed yet again while the rotary bored through a two-hundred-foot-long snow slide. *I won't be getting back to Anchorage or Seward tonight,* Mac decided at the end of day two, for the train was now marooned midway between the two communities.

Mac and the other passengers napped as best they could while the rotary plow worked through the night. In the morning the conductor told him the snow-eating brute had been derailed by the snow and ice, but was back on track.

Not sure when I'll get back to Anchorage, Mac accepted at the end of day three, for that afternoon the plow left the train at mile 52 to clear drifts on northward.

Sitting on the snowbound train Mac looked out at sheer whiteness surrounding him. Snow blanketed everything from the towering mountains to the valley floor, including the now insignificant train. *Not frightening,* he thought, *but peaceful and invigorating. For most folks this string of days will blend in with the endless stream of mundane weeks that make up their unremarkable lives. For me this is just one more Alaskan adventure I'll remember until the end of my days.*

During the long night Mac visited with the conductor between naps. "I'm concerned about this railroad," said the conductor. "Will we ever be able to move trains through this snowy country in the winter?"

Mac tried to sound more confident than he really was. "No reason why we shouldn't be able to. First, we have to learn where all the slide zones are, but I'm working on that right now."

"Knowing where the snow is going to slide won't stop it from avalanching down across the tracks."

"We can't stop the slides," said Mac, "but we can build snow sheds over the track."

"Let's hope the Congress doesn't give up on this railroad before we get these problems worked out."

"The problem with the Congress," said Mac, "is that it's a lot like that big hole under the outhouse; everyone contributes something but most of it stinks."

Mac was exhausted when the delayed train finally reached Kern at midday on the 11th and after clearing one last snow slide was in Anchorage at 9:30 p.m. after a five-day trip from Seward. On his way up to the bunkhouse for some long-awaited rest Mac cataloged yet another Alaskan railroading lesson: *Snow plows and snow sheds will help but when Old Man Winter and Mother Nature get to dancing they can fling out weather that'll test the mettle of this railroad.*

Mac worked alongside the maintenance crews throughout the month as they cleared snow and ice away from the Seward line. He compiled a list of established avalanche chutes and made careful notes on the location of icing and other winter hazards along the mountainous route.

"The Seward line is in good shape," Mac reported to Colonel Mears on the last day of February. "This month came in with a vengeance but it ended just fine and dandy."

Mears expression was probing. "So do you think we'll be able to operate through this country in the winter?"

"We just did! The passenger train from Seward left at 8:15 this morning arrived in Anchorage at 3:30 this afternoon, the fastest time ever between the two towns."

Freight Team in Winter

Frederick C. Mears Papers,
UAF-1984-75-19, Archives, University of Alaska Fairbanks

Chapter Thirty-seven

"The calendar and the thermometer are squabbling again," said Mac as he strode into the boss's office, "one says March and the other says winter."

Mears looked up at Mac from behind his desk, where he was sorting a large stack of paper in equally ominous piles. "Now that we are starting to look like a railroad some think we can coast to the finish line, but we still have over one hundred miles of rail line and five big bridges to build, and at the same time deal with the continuing onslaught of criticism." His gesture toward one of the new paper mountains said it was the complaint pile.

Mac was surprised by the large number of complaints. "Washington is still behind this project aren't they?"

"Depends on the day, and who they are listening to. That self-appointed critic of ours in Seward continues to alter reality at will to discredit the Commission's efforts, and occasionally someone actually listens to him."

"One of the Seward folks told me Mr. Ballaine has a friend up here at the railroad who feeds him information."

"I've heard that too," said Mears. "It'd be nice if we could find out who it is."

Mac acknowledged the assignment with a silent nod, before saying, "I'm told that even Representative Wickersham has been critical of the Commission."

Mears eyes narrowed. "Judge Wickersham has been real vocal about the fact that we aren't yet profitable. But we certainly won't be generating much profit with a half-finished rail system so my top priority is to complete construction of this railroad. We'll push the rail line on up to Hurricane Gulch this summer, but to do that we have to get over fifteen hundred tons of material moved up to the work sites before the snow melts."

"They started moving that stuff up to the end of the line just north of Talkeetna back in January," said Mac. "And teamsters are distributing it to supply points between there and Hurricane Gulch. They should have everything in place before spring."

When Mears said, "But we need to be sure," Mac knew that he was the part of 'we' that would spend the balance of the winter season up north doing the assuring.

Mac arrived at the rail head just as a warmly dressed man was preparing to head north with a four-ton load of spikes. "Fine looking team," said Mac to the driver as he looked up at the large draft animals. "How's the trail looking?"

"Snowy and cold, just the way we like it."

"Mind if I ride along?" Mac asked. "Mears told me to get up here and help out until the job is done."

"Always glad to have an extra hand. Grab your gear and hop on up."

Mac admired the driver's skill as he coaxed the team and the weighty load up the gently rising trail. The Susitna River valley narrowed as they followed along the east bank of the now frozen river.

The big teamster looked out through the fur ruff surrounding the hood of his heavy coat. "The first load of freight arrived at Hurricane on January 30th and we soon had twenty teams working, four horses to a team. We were just getting started when the big storm hit and it was several days before we had the trail back open again."

"The storm caught me down on the Seward line."

The driver carefully held the long leather lines in his heavy mittens as he watched the big horses pull them steadily up the trail. "Been that kind of a winter."

When they reached the Indian River the driver brought the team to a halt. "From here on the trail gets steep, so we need to take this load down to three tons before we start the climb up through the Indian River Valley and then on up to the Hurricane Gulch construction camp." Mac was familiar with the Indian River Valley, confining even without snow, and this year the snow was exceptionally deep and got deeper as they moved northward.

In the following weeks Mac helped the drivers keep the freight moving. Each day he bundled up in heavy clothes topped by his wolf-skin hat and harnessed teams and loaded the sleds. When a driver needed a rest Mac drove their team, and after each snowfall he helped break a new trail. The hard work left little free time, but his mind often wandered back to Anchorage.

Week after week Mac watched the tonnage tally increase and by the time he returned to Anchorage in mid-April seventeen hundred and seventy-three tons of freight was in position and all was ready for the new construction season.

"Time to start thinking about summer," said Toot as he and Mac walked along the muddy street. It was the breakup season in Anchorage, the between season when the landscape was yet bleak but the melt was on. The improving weather, combined with a pay increase at the beginning of April, had railroader's spirits on the rise.

"One of these summers I'll build a house over on that lot I bought back in the 1915 auction," said Mac. "Looks like this town is going to take hold and I don't want to spend the rest of my life in the bunkhouse you know."

"You planning to live there all by yerself, Mac?" asked Toot.

"Don't know yet," said Mac, after a long period of silence.

Toot followed that with a look and a tone that he saved for serious talk. "Well here's my two cents worth. That young lady has cured your bottle fever, so you'd be a damn fool to let her get away."

The palace of meetings this is Mac thought, sitting in the Gee-Oh-Bee with a room full of engineers talking about the steel bridges that would complete the rail system.

Noted bridge engineer W. E. Angier was in Alaska to help Commission engineers make plans for the five bridges, and Mears had thrown Mac into the cluster. "I want you to live and breathe bridges," Mears had said when he'd told Mac that he'd now be monitoring bridge construction. "The big bridges are the key to finishing the rail system, the links that will tie it all together."

Mac listened closely as the engineers explained the unique challenges of each of the five crossings. Crews were already building the approaches to the Susitna River Bridge, and would soon start on the bulky concrete piers that would have to withstand the forces of the ice-choked river each spring. The stream at Hurricane Gulch was relatively small but the chasm was large and the bridge would be nearly three hundred feet above the stream, and the ravine at Riley Creek would require another high bridge. Steel to build the Nenana River bridge at mile 307 would be ordered as soon as Angier and Commission bridge engineer Fogelstrom finished their design. The bridge over the Tanana River near the town of Nenana would be the final link in the system.

Eventually the room full of brains focused on how to assure that each bridge was properly designed and built. Mac listened patiently as the group discussed every detail and every "what if" more times than seemed necessary to his way of thinking. Finally, he said. "Seems to me we're making this way too complicated. My good friend Oleg, bless his soul, once told me that in Russia they just make sure that the chief designer and chief builder know that they'll be standing under the damn bridge when the first train rolls over."

"Colonel Mears is throwing out the first pitch," Mac told Jake as they made their way to the Anchorage baseball park for the opening game of the 1920 season. It was a beautiful day, a Sunday, the 30th of May, and a large crowd was gathering to watch the Commission team take on Company B of the 21st Infantry, who'd been stationed in Anchorage since the prior November.

"Well let's hope this game is more honest than that World Series was last fall," said Jake. "I agree with those who say the fix was in before the first game was played. Ain't no other way to explain how the White Sox played."

As he and Jake seated themselves on the bluff above the ball diamond Mac asked, "What are you and what's left of the Damn Yankees going to do when this railroad is finished?"

Jake gazed down the inlet, toward the rich waters far beyond his view. "Sven has saved most every nickel the railroad paid him, and that will pay for the fishing boat he wants so I expect he'll stay in Alaska and make a living doing what he loves most. That'll make him happier than, as he puts it, 'dat pig vith da shits.'"

"What about the rest of the crew?"

"Paddy hasn't decided yet, and Hans is hiding in the woods up Talkeetna way."

Mac looked directly into Jake's good eye. "We both know that the big bet he placed on the World Series last fall didn't pan out and left him deep in debt to those gambling goons. Then he doubled down by betting on when the ice would go off the river up at Nenana this spring, and now he owes them even more."

Jake tilted his head and looked back at Mac. "And that gang of thugs has some nasty ways of collecting debts, so I expect that's why we haven't seen him. Let's hope he's still alive."

"Hans can take care of himself," said Mac.

The men watched the game in silence for a time, then Mac asked, "What are your plans Jake? You've done a fine job managing the bunkhouse every winter, and your Chamber of Commerce work has been good for our business and good for the community too. Our boarding house business is now well established in this fast growing town, and while Toot and I watch the business when you're out of town we all know that you are the motivating force behind our success."

"I've become real attached to Anchorage and I like being my own boss, and I've made many good friends at the Chamber. I've actually learned to enjoy working with the public."

Mac sized up his partner. "You've changed a lot since you and Toot showed up at Ship Creek five years ago."

"You're right about that," said Jake. "I've adjusted to the climate and I've learned that Alaskans are more concerned about my character than which way my eyes point."

Payne Party at End of Steel, July 17, 1920

Chapter Thirty-eight

"One of the boys ran across some stuff you may be interested in," said Toot as he handed Mac a thick folder.

Mac looked at the bulging portfolio without opening it. "What the hell is it?"

"Seems Mr. Nigel has kept copies of the correspondence with his pen pal in Seward."

"Where did you get this?" asked Mac.

"It was given to me by a friend who works at Nigel's numbers factory. I didn't ask how he got it and I ain't planning to. And, I ain't telling him where it went, and I ain't going to ask you what you plan to do with it. And that's all I'm saying about that," Toot said as he turned and marched away.

In the privacy of his room Mac read through the documents confirming what he'd long suspected about Nigel LeCount. *Probably nothing illegal here, but the misguided scoundrel clearly has an ax to grind with Mr. Mears, and with this railroad.* Mac tossed and turned through the night while coming to a decision on what to do with the damning evidence.

When Mac strode into his office unannounced the next morning Nigel looked out from under his eyeshade, surprised. "Do you have an appointment?"

Mac ignored the question and squeezed his tall frame into the small chair in front of Nigel's desk. He'd heard that Nigel kept the short-legged chair in front of his desk so his visitors would have to look up at him. The typically unflappable bureaucrat suddenly appeared flappable when Mac held up the folder.

"I've come across some information here. Seems that you are helping those who want to discredit Mr. Mears, and this project. And since I'm part of this project I take this very personally."

Nigel clutched the edge of his desk with his claw-like fingers. "I'll fire the son-of-a-bitch who gave that to you." The accountant's face reddened as he glared at Mac. "I demand that you return my property to me immediately!"

The irate man fumed in silence as Mac calmly thumbed through the documents, making sure Nigel knew exactly what he had. "You aren't in much of a position to be making demands Mr. Nigel. But I will give it back to you, by mail, just as soon as you get yourself an address that doesn't end with 'Alaska.'"

"I will get even with you," Nigel shrieked as Mac walked out of the office.

When Interior Secretary Lane was replaced by John Payne that spring Mac watched Mr. Mears work diligently to keep the new Secretary informed about the project, but Payne was soon entangled in the railroad conflicts.

"Now that we've selected the site for the permanent steel bridge over the Tanana," said Mears, "the local commercial clubs are putting pressure on the new Interior Secretary to expedite construction of the new bridge by immediately shipping the steel to Nenana via the Yukon River."

"Self-interest generally comes first in most of these Alaska towns," said Mac.

"But that bridge hasn't even been designed yet, and when we're ready to build it we'll be able to ship the steel up on our own railroad."

"But now you're confusing logic with politics again."

Mears chuckled at that. "You're right. But now that the Fairbanks folks have gone to Mr. Payne with their complaints I'll have to explain it all to him. Hopefully he'll understand."

Mac soon learned that despite the best efforts of Mr. Mears, Secretary Payne had decided to conduct his own investigation of Commission activities. "He announced that he is coming to Alaska," said Mr. Mears, "along with Navy Secretary Josephus Daniels and Rear Admiral Hugh Rodman. The party will leave Seattle about July 10th aboard a fleet of six destroyers. We need the new Secretary's backing to get this project completed, so we want him to leave Alaska with a favorable impression."

"Anything in particular you want him to see?" asked Mac.

"We'll show him anything he wants to see. Most of the criticism is politically motivated and often based on rumor. The best answer to a rumor is the truth, so we'll simply tell them the absolute truth about everything."

Mac was among the crowd of well-wishers in Seward to greet the dignitaries, who'd already been greeted by the beauty of Resurrection Bay and the surrounding mountains and glaciers. As he listened to the speeches delivered from the back of the train that would take the group to Anchorage Mac sized up the entourage of assistants accompanying the group and thought about the advice he'd received from Mears. *Busy executives like Secretary Payne don't have the time to focus on all the details so they rely heavily on their assistants for advice. We need to enlighten Payne, but his assistants will pass their impressions on to their boss so we also need to be sure they fully understand this project.*

When the train prepared to depart Mac climbed aboard and took a seat next to Secretary Payne's aide. He extended his hand and said, "I'm Mac," as they slowly pulled away from the Seward depot.

The carefully groomed young man shook Mac's hand. "My parents named me Cleveland I'm afraid, but I'm called Cleve."

"Pleased to meet you, Cleve," said Mac. "Welcome to Alaska." Mac saw that the obviously serious and intelligent young man was decked out in sharply pressed outdoor garb so new it looked out of place, but he liked his engaging manner and friendly smile.

"Everything is so fresh up here," Cleve said, taking a deep breath. "I don't believe I've ever enjoyed such pure air."

As they rolled along the Snow River Mac pointed out a moose with her calf grazing in the marshy lands adjacent to the rail line. "We take many things for granted I'm afraid."

Cleve watched intently while Mac continued to describe the many wonders of Alaska as the steel road climbed through rich forest land. As the train moved through the towering mountains the Washingtonian said, "You are fortunate to live in such beautiful country. I've had little opportunity to experience wilderness, except for Rock Creek Park."

"I am fortunate," said Mac. "But while the country is beautiful and unthreatening this time of year it becomes more challenging in winter. In fact, the trip that will take us a few hours today took me five days just last February." Though Mac assumed the man's un-calloused hands had never gripped the handle of a snow shovel, he noted that Cleve listened intently while he told how the passengers and crew had plowed and shoveled for five days to get through to Anchorage.

"This is harsh land," said Cleve, "with strong people."

"The good people who live up here have to be strong to face the challenges of daily living," said Mac. He pointed out the engineering challenges they'd faced as they passed through the loop area, where the rail line made a 360-degree loop on a roller-coaster-like wooden trestle to transit the dramatic elevation change. Along the shores of Turnagain Arm he described the construction challenges they had faced when building the line through the rocky slopes.

Mac listened from the back of the room as Mr. Mears briefed the visitors. Standing before a large map of the rail route, pointer in hand, Mears summarized the progress to date, and then focused on the work yet to be done.

"There are about one hundred miles of rail line to be built, and the five large bridges. The Susitna Bridge is already under construction and Hurricane Gulch will be bridged next summer. The Riley Creek and Nenana River bridges should be completed in early 1922 and the Tanana River Bridge will be the last to be built." At the conclusion of his presentation Mears said with sincerity, "I'll be glad to answer any questions you have."

"It has been reported that you wasted a lot of money building track and wooden bridges up near Nenana, only to have them wash away in the spring runoff?"

Mears looked directly at the official who had raised the question. "We have made some mistakes, and that was one of them."

"We've heard that the federal government's fiscal cycle may have slowed progress and increased cost. Is that true?"

"Yes. From the perspective of our construction cycle the federal funding cycle is ass-backwards."

"We know that Alaska has long winters, but so do many of the northern states. Why is weather such a problem for this railroad?"

"The problems are similar, but they are accentuated in Alaska. Our high precipitation levels combined with extreme cold produces avalanches, and the lifting power of freezing moisture often distorts our track. In winter the extreme tides along Turnagain Arm create a river of flowing ice that tears at the slopes along our railroad, and the ice going out of the Susitna River in the spring has the capacity to destroy the railway adjacent to the riverbank. In midwinter we get brief thaws which build up ice in the flangeway and over the rails."

As Mears spoke, Mac noted that his audience was paying close attention to his words.

Mears continued, speaking slowly and confidently. "Because it is easier to move material via sled than to build wagon roads through muskeg we try to take advantage of winter conditions to move supplies to construction sites, but those winter conditions can be difficult as well. For example, when we were hauling material from the head of the Indian River up to the Broad Pass area this past winter there was an average of ten feet of snow on the ground, and single storms would drop five to six feet of new snow."

"They're listening," Mac whispered to Mears as they left the room after the briefing.

"I thought so too," said Mears, still in serious mode.

"Why didn't you mention that you were away in France when Browne built the line that washed out?"

"Because attempts to pass blame, even when valid, make one look weak and irresponsible."

Over the subsequent three days the group inspected the rail line and the Matanuska coal mines, and rode the Commission's power boat up the Susitna River. It became clear to Mac on the train ride back to Anchorage that Cleve had learned much about Alaska. The now voguishly rumpled and slightly smudged man said, "Sweltering heat and high humidity are a summer feature in Washington, but snow and freezing temperatures are relatively rare, sub-zero temperatures are unheard of and minus fifty degree temperatures are unimaginable. I can't fathom working outdoors in that weather."

"It is not an easy job," said Mac. "Steel becomes brittle, machines don't want to work and exposed skin freezes in a matter of seconds."

"You have obviously adapted to this country, Mac, and are dedicated to Alaska and this railroad project," said Cleve, "but I wonder what makes a man like Mr. Mears takes on a challenge of this magnitude."

"Because anything less challenging would bore him."

"Do the workers respect him?"

"They do. He's honest and he cares about them and they know it. I think even the critics of this project respect him, though their statements often don't show it. But Mears tries to avoid the political fray."

"That can be risky," said Cleve. "Partisan rhetoric is always self-serving and often fallacious, but if it goes unchallenged people may accept it as the truth. And remember, Plato warned us that one of the penalties for refusing to participate in politics is that you end up being governed by your inferiors."

"We did all we could to address their concerns" said Mears as he and Mac watched the destroyer 275, with the inspection party aboard, steam away into the milky Cook Inlet waters.

"I think we did a fine job," said Mac. "Even Poetic Pete seems to agree."

> 'Tis a sure sign of spring when all the birds sing,
> And Government folks come to Alaska.
> They come to beat the Washington heat.
> Their pockets filled with taxpayer's moolah.

We take them sightseeing, we take them fishing,
We hold their hand and kiss their ass.
We sell our souls to meet our goals,
And gladly take that government cash.

Mac knew that Secretary Payne had come to Alaska to assess the validity of the negative reports that kept surfacing in Washington and he was confident the Secretary had left with a better understanding of the Alaska project and a favorable impression of Colonel Mears. Mac's confidence was validated when the official report on the Secretary's inspection was issued, refuting the rumors of widespread corruption and mismanagement. *Written by his staff,* Mac guessed.

Susitna River Bridge Construction December 8, 1920

H.G. Kaiser, Alaska Railroad Collection; Anchorage Museum,
B1979.002.AEC.G1690

Chapter Thirty-nine

The year that started rough smoothed out as the construction season progressed. Track laying gangs were extending the rail line steadily northward from Talkeetna while the Damn Yankees and similar crews with different names were clearing and grading on ahead. The flu epidemic that had killed some seventy-five people in Nenana that spring had passed and with the crews back at work the track was soon in place down to the construction camp at Healy and work had begun in the Nenana River Canyon.

On a midsummers day when the news was all good it got even better when Mears said to Mac, "Nigel is gone."

Mac tried to act surprised when he asked, "Permanently gone?"

"Gone for good! He wanted to transfer back to Washington and I supported the idea."

The tinge of guilt Mac felt passed in an instant. "He'll fit in well back there."

When the steel for the Susitna River Bridge arrived in Anchorage Mac prepared to head north to monitor construction of the concrete piers that would support the bridge. "Early on I under-estimated the Susitna's power," said Mears as he and Mac studied the blueprints spread across the engineering table. "But, when I visited that area during the spring breakup and saw the power of the ice-filled river I realized that we would not be able to put piers in the waterway."

Mac took one last look at the design for the huge concrete structures. "I plan to stay up there until these shore-side founda-tions are done."

"Take that winter hat of yours with you," said Mears. "You're going to need it."

The gray skies hinted of winter though no snow had yet fallen in the valleys. Mac typically looked for Mt. McKinley on the northbound train trip, but with even the lower peaks shrouded in low-hanging clouds he watched the nearby scenery slip silently by, and got a history lesson.

"Concrete, one of mankind's greatest inventions," said Plumb-bob, who was on his way up to the bridge site to check on the concrete mixing process. "This stuff was used extensively by the ancient Romans to build bridges, aqueducts and of course the Pantheon—"

Of course.

"and many of those structures are still here today."

"Just a mixture of gravel, sand, cement and water, right?"

"In the proper proportions."

"But with winter just around the corner everything will be frozen solid real soon," said Mac.

"You wear that old wolf on your head to keep your ears warm in winter and we'll come up with a way to keep the concrete warm in the winter too."

The foreman greeted them when they arrived at the bridge site. "Seems this project keeps forcing us to invent new ways to build in this cold country."

"I've already signed off on the procedure for heating the sand, gravel, cement and water," said Plumb-bob, "but I still have some questions about how we're going insulate the pier forms."

Mac held the dumb end of the measuring tape while the engineer made measurements and drawings and notes. By the end of the second day Mac was unsure if the cloud around the engineer's head was vapor from his breath or smoke from his engineer brain.

Finally, Plumb-bob delivered a plan, a documented and detailed process for lining the pier forms with heavy canvas, and then keeping heat on the concrete while it cured. The next day Plumb-bob waved good-bye to Mac and the construction foreman as he boarded the southbound train for Anchorage.

"Follow the process we've established and you'll have piers that will hold this bridge up for many years."

Mac worked alongside the crew, making sure they followed Plumb-bob's instructions. He was pleased to see that even as the daily temperatures descended the yards-poured tally climbed. The log bunkhouse where Mac lived along with the other workers was a temporary structure that matched the theme of other crew quarters along the line. The bunks were hard but a well fed stove kept the inside temperature livable.

Each morning as they trudged out the door, the bundled men gauged the friendliness of the day by the thickness of the frost and the bite in the air, and then validated their suspicions by glancing at the thermometer nailed to a nearby tree. Most would walk silently on as though they hadn't noticed but eventually someone would proudly announce the reading.

"Twenty-five below this morning."

The temperature continued to drop but the first piers were taking shape, getting taller and heavier each day, and the work continued even when the red mercury in the thermometer dropped to the minus forty-two-degree mark.

When Mac returned to Anchorage late that year he was able to report that the piers were in place on both sides of the frozen river and the American Bridge Company crews had begun erecting the steel for the superstructure.

The good news was welcomed in the offices of the Gee-Oh-Bee and stove side at the NEW Bunkhouse Royale. "Vill dey get dat bridge up dis vinter?" asked Sven.

"They will," said Mac, and then asked, "What are you boys doing to stay out of trouble this winter?"

"Paddy took a railroad job and Hans is permanently lost in the woods up north of Talkeetna," said Jake.

The other men surrounding the stove showed no concern, but Mac had to ask. "What do you mean by permanently lost?"

"He's tired of being hounded about his gambling debts so he got his name added to the list of folks who died in the flu epidemic and headed off into the woods. If you follow the ravine running off to the east just beyond mile 244 you'll find a little lake and cabin. The fella living there looks a lot like Hans, but he goes by the name of Braunschweiger Johnson."

Mac's face remained dead serious. "Let's hope that keeps the debt collector away."

"If that gangster had any sense he'd stay away from Hans," said Jake, "but those thugs ain't known for being smart."

And Hans isn't exactly known for being chicken-livered, thought Mac, before saying to Jake. "So that leaves you. What are your winter plans, besides running the bunkhouse?"

"I'm fixin to get back to my civic duties."

"Are you running for mayor?"

"That ain't as funny as you think," said Jake. "The railroad doesn't want to be responsible for this town any longer and most of us think the Anchorage citizens can manage their own town just fine."

When the self-management question was brought to a vote Mac was surprised to learn that it was defeated. "Doesn't seem logical," he said to Mears. "Everyone I know wants this town to be independent from the railroad."

"I think the ballots will show that, if they're counted properly," said Mears. "A Seattle judge declared that the proposal was defeated, but I've discovered that eighty-five blank ballots were counted as opposed to the incorporation of the city."

Mac was aghast. "But blank ballots aren't for or against."

"That's what I think," said Mears, "and I've contacted the district attorney to make the argument that those ballots shouldn't be counted at all."

The validity of Mears' argument was confirmed when the judge reversed his decision and threw out the blank ballots. The November 23, 1920 incorporation of Anchorage launched the town that had been designed and hatched by the Alaska Engineering Commission only five years prior on the journey that would make it the population and commercial center of Alaska.

When Mac learned that on December 1st the operation and maintenance of the town would be turned over to city authorities, he said to Toot, "Now we need to get a mayor."

Toot grinned and said, "Poetic Pete has already mentioned that."

"There'll be no doxies on our streets,"
The railroad said of their town so fair.
"And there'll be no booze and no card cheats,
Though we may allow a house of prayer."

It'd be a fine town they did believe,
Yet there came a lady whose luck had run down.
She lived in town by day, but in the eve,
She plied her trade just out of town.

She was a jolly soul and finely buxom,
So she gathered friends both day and night.
Her night-time friends by day were mum,
But everyone in town thought her a total delight.

Then the railroad said, "Our worries are quelled,
We'll no longer be the town's purveyor."
So the citizens took charge and elections were held.
Now the lady of the night is called Madam Mayor!

"Rumor of the week is that the cost of this railroad is going up again," said Toot to Mac on a December Saturday, as the men lingered by the kitchen table at mid-morning waiting for the sun to come up.

"It's true," said Mac. "The Commission says that in addition to the fifty-two million dollars already authorized, another three-and-a-half million will be needed to complete the entire project and provide for maintenance and operation up to the date of completion."

With question marks all over his face Toot said, "Seems like we're near done now."

"We are. The new rail line reaches from Seward north to mile 275. On the north end there is narrow gauge service from Fairbanks down to North Nenana, and the new line extends from Nenana south to mile 358. The eighty-three-mile gap between the ends of steel has all been cleared and thirty-three miles has been graded. The rail line will be done next year, but it'll take another year after that to finish the bridges."

Ice Damage Along Susitna River

H.G. Kaiser, Alaska Railroad Collection; Anchorage Museum,
B1979.002.AEC.G1751

Chapter Forty

In the opening month of 1921 the critical item on the railroad's construction schedule was the bridge over the Susitna River, where workers were struggling to assemble the steel structure in the bitter cold. But, Mac also knew that it was the time when the hard frozen river gave the builders a solid platform to work from, for the thick ice supported timber falseworks, which in turn supported the heavy steel structure during the construction process.

In early February Mac accompanied Mr. Mears on a trip to the bridge site to witness the opening of the new structure. The crisscrossed wooden falseworks were removed on the 2nd, and the jubilant Mears watched the first train roll across the bridge just four days later. "The rail line can now be extended on to Hurricane Gulch."

Mac, too, was already looking ahead. "And the foundation work is already underway. And that's good because it'll take a hellacious pile of concrete to hold the heavy steel arch that's going to carry our rail line through the thin air above that near bottomless ravine."

Jawing away the time on the train ride back to Anchorage Mears and Mac rehashed Warren G. Harding's victory in the November election. "Seemed like he wouldn't even get nominated," said Mac, "then he went and won the election."

Mears looked out at the winter whiteness. "Now he'll soon be sworn in as the 29th President of the United States, and that means there will soon be a new Interior Secretary overseeing the Alaska Engineering Commission."

"One more new boss," said Mac, leaning back in his seat. "What do we need to do the get ready for this one?"

"First thing I'm going to do is generate public support for this project, so I'll soon be heading south on a speaking tour."

While Mears was gone Mac followed the news reports telling how Mears was entertaining eager audiences in Seattle and Portland by narrating moving pictures of the government railroad in Alaska, always giving credit to the workers. They reported that while Mears expressed his confidence in the value of developing Alaska he also cautioned that it had taken two to three decades to develop the American West and the development of remote Alaska would require even more time.

By mid-April Mac was able to report that, "The crews will be ready to start the steel work on the Hurricane Gulch bridge just as soon as the rail line gets there."

"I'm glad things are going well on the construction side," said Mears, "because maintaining this railroad has been a challenge this winter. Just this morning the southernmost span of the bridge at mile 49.3 was destroyed by a huge snow slide that carried away part of the bridge, two engines, a rotary plow and two cabooses. There were no serious injuries, but it'll take weeks to get that line reopened."

When the ice went out on the Susitna River just a few weeks later the powerful jams forced the ice up over the bank, destroying the rail line at mile 237, and again the line was closed for several days while repairs were made.

The fat cook methodically cleared away the breakfast dishes as the men sitting around the table enjoyed an extra cup of coffee on a Saturday morning. Mac looked at Toot, sensing that with the snow gone his friend was looking forward to getting outside.

"I could use some good carpenter advice. Thought maybe we could take a little walk and look at some of the houses in this town, maybe find one that would look good on that lot of mine."

Toot beamed. "Partner, sounds like your nesting instincts are getting the best of you this spring."

The men finished their coffee, hatted up and struck out into the beautiful day, the sun's warmth quickly erasing any residual ghosts of the just-ended winter.

"I expect that one day this town will grow out beyond these alphabet streets," Toot speculated as they started off across Anchorage, walking southward, away from the city center.

Mac looked up and down the orderly streets. "This town is proving to be entirely capable of self-governance. Everywhere I look I see the unbridled enthusiasm that accompanies independence. The citizens are determined to build a model community and Jake and his Chamber of Commerce friends have grand plans for the future of Anchorage, headquarters of the soon-to-be-competed government railroad."

"How big a house you planning to build?" asked Toot.

"Just a small place," said Mac, pointing out a cozy looking bungalow. The little house that had caught Mac's eye sat peacefully on a perfectly rectangular lot along one of the perfectly rectangular city blocks laid out by the engineers back in 1915. The white picket fence enclosed a well-tended yard and a well-maintained house. The dormers on the steeply pitched roof suggested that cozy bedrooms were tucked beneath and the kitchen window overlooked the tidy back yard. A small covered porch welcomed residents and guests and protected the entry from the winter snowfall.

"Nice little house," said Toot. For the balance of the morning they strolled along the Anchorage streets looking at homes and visiting with the many residents out cleaning the winter's accumulation of dirt and trash from their yards. As their stroll ended Toot said, "I think that little bungalow is the perfect design for you, Mac. You planning to build this summer?"

"I'd like to know what's going to happen to my job before I start building. I want to stay with the railroad but I doubt that Mears will need an assistant once the construction work is done. Besides that, I'll be up at Hurricane most of this summer, helping get that bridge built."

"That's going to be one hell of a bridge."

Hurricane Gulch Bridge August 8, 1921

H.G. Kaiser, Alaska Railroad Collection; Anchorage Museum,
B1979.002.AEC.G1885

Chapter Forty-one

I'll be needing a double dose of energy from you this year thought Mac, glancing up at the summer sun. The bright summer orb was every Alaskan's friend but with bridges to build he was certain the season of endless sunshine would pass all too quickly. Today, Mac prepared to return to Hurricane. The thirty-five hundred cubic yards of concrete that would support the bridge were nearly in place and the American Bridge Company was ready to start erecting the steel arch.

Mears was intense when he said to Mac, "Keep the project on schedule. Our critics have been working overtime again and they will use any delay as a reason to continue their assault on us."

Mac did not bring it up, but he knew the Commission's appropriation had faced serious challenges in Congress that spring, with attention being focused on increasing cost and management of the project. A request to increase Mears' salary from ten to fifteen thousand dollars had fanned the flames of controversy.

"And," said Mears, "Albert Fall, the new Interior Secretary, expects to see results."

Mac looked squarely at his boss. "We'll have trains running over the gulch in August, and the grading crews are already working north of the bridge site."

Up at Hurricane Mac found that the bridge had sprouted from the piers attached to the rock walls. *This can't possibly work* the voices in his head told him as he looked up at the steel arch emerging simultaneously from both canyon walls. *I know the engineers*

have made the calculations but this defies common sense, and possibly the laws of physics as well. I understand how the two sides of the arch will support one another when joined together in the middle, but what the hell holds them up there in mid-air until then? From his vantage point on the valley floor three hundred feet below he could see workers crawling around on the seemingly flimsy steel. As piece after piece of steel was lowered to the fearless workers they secured them to the growing structure.

It's like an igloo Mac realized one July day. *If you can keep the walls from collapsing until you get the cap block in the center you will have an indestructible dome. But the closer you get to the top the more likely the structure is to collapse.*

The idea that the under-construction bridge might collapse like an unfinished igloo haunted Mac through the long summer days as he watched the two halves advance steadily toward the center point. He recalled that when they'd started pouring the first pier for the Susitna bridge the humus in the gravel had weakened the concrete, leading to a partial collapse of the structure. The problem had been resolved, but the incident gave Mears' critics one more thing to complain about, and had shown that mistakes are possible.

As August rolled around the bridge halves were each perilously far from the anchoring canyon sidewall, but to Mac's great relief the two dangling half-arcs were joined on August 10th. Work was immediately started on the north approach structure and on August 15th the first work train passed over the bridge. *Two up, three to go,* thought Mac as he watched the first regular train travel over the bridge just three days later.

Later in the week, just as Jake and Sven, the last of the Damn Yankees, were returning from a long day of work, Mac moseyed into their construction camp as though he lived in the neighborhood. "Evening fellas, just came in on the Caterpillar train so thought I'd drop by for a bite to eat." With the bridge open Mac had traveled north from Hurricane on one of the short strings of freight wagons being pulled over the wagon road by a Caterpillar tractor, moving men and materials to the Broad Pass area where construction gangs were hard at work.

"We're just getting ready to cook up some hard beans and dry moose steak," said Jake, clearly pleased to see his friend and business partner.

Mac responded to that one with a laugh. "Makes a person look forward to the international cuisine back at the bunkhouse."

"It does," said Jake, laughing along with him. "But I'll bet you didn't come clear up here just to get some good campfire food."

"Just taking a quick look at how things are going up on this end before I head back to Anchorage. Colonel Mears will want all of the details."

"He ought to be happy," said Jake. "Us contractors have worked ourselves out of business."

"Yah, dis vill be our last yob on dis railroad," said Sven.

Jake put a match to the kindling in the rock fire ring and watched thoughtfully as the flames slowly took hold. "After we finish this last contract we'll turn in our equipment, collect our last pay check and be finished."

"Yah sure, but da finish is yust da beginning."

"That's a good way to put it," said Jake. "Sven plans to become part of the new Alaska. He's going to settle along Kachemak Bay and spend the rest of his years fishing the rich Alaskan waters."

As the camp fire came to life Jake set the pot of beans on the grill. "Hans ... Braunschweiger Johnson, is hanging out at his cabin up north of Talkeetna for now, but I expect he'll take seasonal work with the railroad after this debt collection problem blows over. Did you see anything of our old partner this summer?"

"Didn't lay eyes on Mr. Johnson, but may have heard about him."

"Vhat are you meaning?"

"Word in Talkeetna this summer was that some lowlife was in town looking for someone named Hans. Wasn't but a week later a body floated ashore along the Susitna River, not far downstream from mile 244."

"Vas dat Hans?"

"It was the collection goon."

"Yah sure. He swimmed like dem rocks."

"The death was called a drowning, but the agents told me the guy's neck was broken before he was thrown into the river."

Jake's face tightened. "So now I reckon they're looking for who done it?"

"Nope. They figure Alaska is better off without the guy, so they're not wasting any time on it."

"They'll have the line pushed through to Riley Creek before year end," Mac reported to Colonel Mears in September. "The grading is nearly complete and rail gangs are laying as much as sixty-six hundred feet of rail in a single day. And, the crews up in the canyon are closing in from the north side as well."

"So we will have the rail line completed later this year?"

"Don't see any reason why not."

When Mac returned north after freeze-up that fall he saw gangs laying temporary track directly on the frozen ground in the Broad Pass to Riley Creek area, rapidly closing the gap between the ends of rail.

At Riley Creek workers were preparing to assemble the steel bridge. The crossing was not nearly as high above the ground as Hurricane so instead of a gravity-defying arch the bridge would be supported on tall steel piers that would spring from the bottom of the ravine.

Reports from up north at the Nenana River said the timber abutments were under construction, as were the foundations for the three truss spans that would bridge the river. The summer had disappeared all too soon, but after years of agonizingly slow progress the final pieces of the system were quickly falling in place, but Mac was torn. *The project that I've worked on for the last eight years is finally ending, but I'm afraid this chapter of my life will end along with it.*

Rail across the ice at Nenana showing type of Locomotive used.
Dec 11th. 21.

Train Crossing Tanana River on Ice

Frederick C. Mears Papers,
UAF-1984-75-31, Archives, University of Alaska Fairbanks

Chapter Forty-two

Mid-afternoon of November 19, 1921, the last piece of rail was spiked in place at mile 347 and except for the unfinished bridges at Riley Creek, the Nenana River and the Tanana River there was a steel road from Seward to Fairbanks. With transfers or ice bridges at the three un-spanned crossings and the use of narrow gauge equipment from Nenana to Fairbanks the railroad could now move freight and passengers from the ports of Seward and Anchorage through to Fairbanks.

"I hear the Chamber is planning a big party to celebrate the almost completion of the railroad." Toot said to Jake.

"Sure as hell are. This is the biggest thing that's happened in this town since we've been a town. We've set up a five-day train trip so we can have a rolling celebration, traveling all the way up to Fairbanks and back."

"A trip for Chamber members only?" asked Toot.

"For Alaskans," said Jake. "You and Mac are going along too."

The celebratory mood on the excursion train engulfed Mac as they pulled out of the Anchorage station on Saturday the 26th of November with a full load of Chamber members, guests and railroad employees aboard. He knew that on this day all were proud of their accomplishment and united in their enthusiasm for the future of the railroad and the future of Alaska.

As they moved slowly along Knik Arm Mac listened to the passenger's marvel at the modern transportation system carrying them through the newly opened country. Crossing the bridges over the frozen Knik and Matanuska rivers a cacophony of voices expressed amazement at the sight of the spired peaks of the surrounding Chugach and Talkeetna Mountains.

"The inspiration of artists."

"Magical and mystical."

"Home of the gods."

Rolling across the Matanuska-Susitna Valley Mac joined Jake and a group of his Chamber associates speculating about the future of their community. "The City of Anchorage is on its own now," Jake pointed out, "but we remain closely tied to the government railroad."

There was a murmur of agreement before one of the men asked, "Mac, do you think Anchorage will always be just a railroad town?"

Mac wrestled with the question before providing his view of the future. "Anchorage started as the stepchild of the railroad, but as we grow we will build our own identity. In time the railroad will be only one of many Anchorage employers."

North of Talkeetna a glimpse of Mt. McKinley set Mac to speculating. *I wonder if Alaska will someday become a tourist destination? Will the bunkhouse someday be converted to a tourist hotel? Will the name be changed from the NEW Bunkhouse Royale to the Ship Creek Beach Resort and Spa? Will we open a second hotel in Talkeetna?*

Passing through the Indian River Valley Mac took note of the deep snow, and contemplated the work it would take to keep the rail line open during the winter months.

Up at Chulitna Toot shared his dreams with Mac and Jake. "I like the B & B work. I've mastered the trade, people respect my abilities and I feel good about the work my crew does to maintain this railroad."

"Sounds like you'll be staying on with the railroad," said Mac.

"I'll be here as long as they need me."

Broad Pass showed its winter splendor to the train load of Alaskans, and at Riley Creek the passengers bundled up and trudged through the snowy ravine to a train waiting on the north side of the unfinished bridge.

As they cleared the Nenana River Canyon Mears asked Mac to join him for a private conversation. Mac's worst fears were validated when, chugging up along the Nenana River Colonel Mears said, "With construction nearly complete I no longer need an assistant."

Mac was determined to remain strong, despite his anguish. "I've been expecting this. How soon do I need to start looking for work?"

"You're not being laid off, Mac. You're being transferred to another job. The Maintenance of Way Department needs a foreman and you're the perfect man for the job. The pay is twenty-four hundred dollars a year and you better than anyone know this railroad will always need maintaining."

Mac sat silently, searching for words. His long-held dream of a truly stable job was finally realized but manliness forbade him from expressing his true feelings. Finally, "So I guess my days as your Horse-Riding Assistant have come to an end."

"Yes, but you'll still need that horse from time to time so she'll go with you to the new job."

"What will happen to the other people who have helped build this railroad, like Plumb-bob and the others?" asked Mac.

"Some will stay on to help operate the railroad, others will move on to other jobs I suppose," said Mears.

When Poetic Pete and an equally unique man came dancing along the aisle of the moving rail car Mac said, "I'm told that Poetic Pete and his cousin plan to open a dance hall up in Fairbanks." While Mears was still looking for words Mac said, "Of course you know Poetic Pete, but let me introduce you to his cousin Pete."

Mac motioned the dancing duo over and said, to the second Pete, "I'd like you to meet Colonel Mears."

Duh-Duh-**DUM**-Dum
Duh-Duh-**DUM**-Dum
Duh-Duh-**DUM**-Dum-Dah-Dah-Dah

How-dy-**HOW**-dy
Nice-to-**MEET**-ya
You-can-**CALL**-me Pol-ka-Pete

I'm-from-**WIS**-consin
Like-to-**POL**-ka
And-I-**TALK**-ina-Pol-ka-Beat.

They went around the unfinished bridge over the Nenana River on a temporary rail line called a shoo-fly, and as they moved on toward the town of Nenana Mac asked Colonel Mears about the railroad's financial future. "Do you think we can generate enough revenue to operate this railway?" he asked.

"There will certainly be financial challenges," said Colonel Mears. "Some folks question whether the new railroad will ever generate enough revenue to justify the government's investment, but others maintain that financial gain is not important because the purpose of the line is to facilitate the development of Alaska."

"Sounds like an argument that won't end soon," said Mac.

"The question is political, so there may never be a clear answer."

Crossing the Tanana River on a rail line atop the ice and transferring to a narrow gauge train reshuffled the passengers, putting Mac in the midst of a group speculating on resource development. "We all know there is still gold to be mined in this country," one said, "and the coal mining business is just getting started."

"In the future," another said, "other resources will be found in this country. These new automobiles run on gasoline, made from oil, and they tell me that oil and coal are often found in the same places."

Mac, Jake and Toot sat together in private conversation on the final leg of the trip, through the Gold Stream Valley to Fairbanks. Mac listened to the rhythmic click-clack of the steel wheels passing over the rail joints as they discussed their past, and their future. *Like the railroad*, he knew, *this partnership was at a critical juncture.*

"Toot is well established in his railroad job and has less and less time to give to our business," said Mac, "and I have a new job at the railroad now, and a house to build."

"Well you won't be spending as much time with that teacher," said Toot. "I hear she is thinking of going back south when the school term ends."

270

Mac's expression signaled his acknowledgment, and his concern.

"You thinking about trying to change her mind?" asked Jake.

"Thinking about it," said Mac, "now that I finally have a real job."

The men rode for several miles in silence before Mac said, "I've been thinking that we should make Jake the managing partner of the NEW Bunkhouse Royale, a full-time job with a salary. This will allow Toot and I to become silent partners and focus on our railroad careers."

"I'll second that," said Toot.

Jake, with a glint in the eye that was now directed at Toot and a serious look pointed toward Mac, said, "I reckon this plan will give you more time for your personal life too."

As they arrived in Fairbanks Mac sat back and reflected on the trip. *We've just made an unprecedented all-rail trip deep into interior Alaska. Communities like Talkeetna, Nenana and Fairbanks are no longer isolated outposts, but regular stops on an all-weather transportation system. The rail line is complete, two of the three remaining bridges are under construction and the railroad is accepting through traffic between Seward and Fairbanks. The government railroad is open for business, but it still doesn't have a name.*

Riley Creek Bridge

Alaska Railroad Collection; Anchorage Museum,
B1979.002.AEC.H139.1

Chapter Forty-three

"Hot flapjacks, special of the day," the fat cook intoned his daily mantra as he plopped a heaping plate of hotcakes on the table.

Mac had just returned from Riley Creek, where the third steel bridge had been completed on February 5th and the wind-driven snow beating at the frosted window made him glad that it was a Sunday so he could relax in the warm kitchen instead of trudging off to work.

"The perfect start for a cold morning," he said, looking at the hot aromatic cakes.

"So what do you expect the name will be?" asked Toot.

"Hotflapjacksspecialoftheday," said Jake, mocking the cook.

Toot didn't crack a smile. "I know what our breakfast is called, same as every other day. I want to know what they will name the government railroad. Word is, now that the line is almost finished the folks back in Washington are going to give it an official name."

Jake looked moody for a moment, perhaps introspective, then said, "I reckon it'll be the Warren G. Harding Line, or some such thing."

"They sure as hell aren't likely to give credit where credit is due," said Toot, pouring maple syrup on the cakes, "like to Mr. Mears. He's the one who built this damn railroad, but they ain't giving him credit for much of anything these days."

Waiting for his chance at the syrup, Mac explained. "Mears has done a great job, but that new Interior Secretary has been bombarded by John Ballaine's continuing efforts to discredit him."

"Most of Alaska is solidly behind Mr. Mears," said Jake. "The support from the Fairbanks Commercial Club and the Anchorage

Chamber has helped persuade Secretary Fall to leave Mears in charge."

"That's true," said Mac, "but Ballaine's campaign to unseat Mears just keeps going. Now he's complaining to Alaska Governor Scott Bone that our freight rates are unfair."

Jabbing the air with his fork Toot poked a hole in that one. "But Mears debunked the accusation by explaining the basis of the rates to Governor Bone."

Mac held up his index finger while he finished chewing the mouth full of pancakes, then said, "True, but Ballaine continues to publish inaccurate information critical of Mears. That man won't be happy unless he gets Mears fired."

Toot stopped chewing, swallowed and tentatively said, "That ain't likely to happen, is it?"

In March Mac reported to the bunkhouse partners that the Secretary of the Interior had selected The Alaska Railroad as the official name of the new line.

"Not a bad choice, nice and simple."

"Kind of makes the railroad the official representative of this great country," said Jake.

Toot endorsed that with his trademark grin. "And in a way that honors all those who came up here to build the railroad, and run it."

"Like the crews who've worked through the winter to get the Nenana crossing finished before the ice goes off the river," said Mac. "Reports I'm getting say they'll be done by mid-April so we'll soon be running freight and passenger service from Seward to Fairbanks."

Toot sighed. "Only as long as the Tanana remains frozen so you can run that funny little train across on the ice."

"Don't worry yourself about that," said Mac. "After the ice goes out the railroad will set up boat service to provide the transfer between the standard gauge line on the south side of the river and the narrow gauge line on the north."

Good news came from every direction that spring and summer, as the last pieces of the puzzle fell in place. On May 9th the railroad announced that the American Bridge Company was awarded the contract to fabricate and build the seven-hundred-foot steel span that would run forty feet above the Tanana River.

Two months later, after the rail line that had been laid on the frozen ground in the Broad Pass area the prior winter was raised, surfaced and ballasted, the railroad began offering twice weekly service between Seward and Nenana. Other improvements were made up and down the railroad; snow sheds on the Seward line and a two-story hotel to provide an overnight stop for travelers at Dead Horse Hill, now named Curry, that included a tennis court, swimming pool and a golf course.

"We'll need to start with a good foundation, just like those bridges you've been building," said Toot to Mac as they started the house building process. This weekend he and Toot were building forms for the foundation. "You best be getting a crew hired to pour concrete."

"Already taken care of. Found some out-of-work station men who are anxious to get started, all damn fine workers. And when the foundation is done they'll start building. We'll turn them loose during the day and you and I can supervise in the evenings, and on weekends."

"That'll work."

Summer waxed and waned but with the help of the used-to-be station men and Toot the new home was finished before the condensed autumn season roared in.

"What color you going to paint this place?" asked Toot as he and Mac stood along the street admiring the new structure.

"White I suppose."

"You suppose! Meaning it ain't exactly your decision?"

"Meaning it'll be invisible as soon as the snow flies and you won't be able to find me."

"Winter, winter, winter, summer, winter, winter, winter again," Toot mumbled as he helped Jake put up storm windows to prepared the bunkhouse for the next cold portion of Alaska's lopsided annual cycle.

Jake handed up the last of the protective seasonal panes. "We're almost done with this little chore, and you'll be glad we have these up when the real cold weather gets here."

"Ain't the same around here now that the Damn Yankees are gone and Mac has moved into his new house," he said as they sat at the big kitchen table for a mid-morning cup of coffee.

"Things are changing," said Jake. "These new residents are long-termers, not here to build this railroad but to run it. I been wondering Jake, since everything is done expect for the bridge over the Tanana, will 1922 go down as the year The Alaska Railroad was completed?"

"No. This has been the year when the line was nearly completed, but it won't be done until you can climb aboard a train in Seward and ride it all the way to Fairbanks. Colonel Mears will have it wrapped up soon, if his critics don't run him off first."

Toot's simmering frustration boiled over. "Why don't they let up on the man? He ain't done a damn thing wrong!"

"I've been thinking," said Jake, looking deep into the cup of black coffee on the table before him. "This is all part of the public process. Every citizen has the right to voice their opinion, and it's the job of elected officials to listen to them all. Of course people's opinions change, and after every election we have new folks in office so my guess is that as long as this railroad is owned by the government that public process and common sense will be fighting over how it ought to be run, and who ought to be running it."

President Harding with Engineer Brayford

Chapter Forty-four

"They fired Mears," said Mac as he burst into the bunkhouse parlor in mid-February surrounded by a cloud of gloom.

Jake looked at Mac in disbelief. "I thought Mears was down in the States?"

Mac shed his hat and coat and took a seat in the still familiar parlor. "He is. I wouldn't be surprised if that's why they picked this particular time to give him the ax."

"Who's they?" asked Toot.

"Interior Secretary Fall started the lynching, but it took a gang of the worthless hacks to finish the job."

"I figured Fall was the one who was going to get fired," said Jake. "That crook ought to go to jail for that Teapot Dome shenanigan he pulled."

"I'm told he knows he's on the way out," said Mac. "So to avoid being fired he announced that he'll soon be vacating his position. Then, as a lame duck, he consolidated the Alaska Engineering Commission with the Alaska Road Commission."

"I ain't sure what the problem is," said Toot. "This government railroad reorganizes itself every so often weather it needs reorganizing or not."

Mac remained dead serious. "I expect Mr. Mears may have been uncertain too, at least until the Army sent him orders relieving him of his duties with the Alaska Engineering Commission and reassigning him to an Army unit in Seattle. Then, on the very same day, Fall notified him that his position is being taken over by James Steese, the chairman of the Alaska Road Commission."

Toot was serious now too. "The chicken-shit sons-a-bitches picked a chicken-shit way to fire the man."

The Tanana River Bridge, the final link in the continuous steel rail line from Seward to Fairbanks, had just been completed when Mears returned to Anchorage at the end of February to conclude his railroad responsibilities. The line from North Nenana to Fairbanks was still narrow gauge, but Mac knew that when the weather broke crews would convert it to standard gauge. Because the narrow gauge Chatanika branch joined the main line at Happy the railroad from there on into Fairbanks would consist of three rails.

The loss of his friend and mentor weighed on Mac that spring as he witnessed the anticlimactic end of railroad construction blend seamlessly in with railroad operations. The railroad's concern about construction costs, which topped out at over fifty-six million dollars, were replaced with concern about profitability. The estimated revenue for the fiscal year ending June 30th covered less than half of the operating cost, and when maintenance expenses were added the railroad's total loss climbed even higher.

The new railroad's financial challenges are just beginning, Mac thought, *but the Alaska Railroad is now ready to tackle those challenges with full scale rail operations. Us folks who work here will no longer be puppets waiting for the politicians and the bureaucrats to pull our string. The future of this railroad is now in our hands.*

"I ain't seen this many folks in one place since that time I went to church on Easter Sunday," Toot pointed out to his bunkhouse partners as they stood in the crowd in front of the Chamber of Commerce building on the evening of July 13, 1923, waiting for the President of the United States to speak.

President Harding had arrived in Seward earlier in the day along with numerous high-ranking government officials, wives, and at least thirty reporters. Mac found some consolation in the news that John Ballaine had been turned away when he attempted to board the special train carrying the presidential party from Seward to Anchorage.

"The man don't look well," Toot whispered to his friends when Mr. Harding stepped to the podium.

"Looks to me like he's suffering from train lag, or boat lag," Jake added. "He's traveled over four thousand miles to get here you know."

"But you can't see straight," said Toot, the least tactful of the three. "Looks to me like a man who has a date with the grim reaper."

The next day Mac, who'd once again been asked to help herd tourists, accompanied the presidential group as they headed north. Near Wasilla the President took the controls of Locomotive 618 and under the direction of engineer Brayford drove the train as far as Willow. After stopping at Montana to allow Mrs. Harding and others to inspect a local flower bed they traveled on to Curry to spend the night.

On Sunday afternoon the gang of sojourners reached North Nenana, site of the golden spike ceremony. Admiral Rodman had advised the reporters to dress in heavy shirts, heavy underwear, sweaters, galoshes and leggings. Like all seasoned Alaskans, Mac knew summer days in the Interior can be very hot, and this was one of those days. Mac watched in amusement as the snuggly dressed experts suffered through the heat and the speeches.

Profound, Mac thought when Steese began his remarks by telling the group what they likely already knew, that they had traveled on a special train, were standing upon the bank of the Tanana and would soon travel on to Fairbanks. *And this is the guy they picked to replace Mr. Mears?*

Mac smiled to himself when Steese concluded his remarks with, "Mr. Secretary, as Chairman of the Alaska Engineering Commission, the construction agency designated by the President to carry out, under your direction, the will of Congress, it is my duty to report to you and, through you, to the President, that the will of Congress, as expressed in the Act of March 12, 1914, has now been accomplished."

Interesting, Mac thought, *that he didn't mention that neither he nor Interior Secretary Work had assumed their present positions until after the railroad had been completed, or that the project had been initiated by President Wilson almost seven years before Harding took office.*

Interior Secretary Work praised those who had built the railroad, and even mentioned Mears' dedication to the project, before handing the ceremonial spike to the President. The golden spike, Mac knew, had been a gift to Colonel Mears and bore the inscription, "To Colonel Frederick Mears, who built the Alaska Railroad from Seward to Fairbanks, from the people of Anchorage."

Late in the afternoon, late in his life, the President of the United States spoke. He paid tribute to those who built the railroad but then reverted to campaign mode, adding that he, "...did not suppose any individual or set of individuals would have undertaken the construction of such a railway, that it had to be left to the government itself."

Governor Bone placed the golden spike in a prepared hole, the President tapped gently, and the spike was removed. An iron spike was then placed in the hole and the President swung the ceremonial maul, and missed.

.

Lady on the Alaska Railroad

Alaska State Library, Alaska Engineering Commission Photographs,
ASL-P559-43

Chapter Forty-five

Mac sat on the bluff above the creek, finding solace in the ebbs and flows of the Cook Inlet waters. *Lifelike,* he thought, for he'd discovered stability in the rhythm of life.

The Ship Creek flats had changed dramatically since he'd sat at this spot some nine years prior awaiting the government railroad builders. The sun still circled in the summer sky and the salmon-filled stream still flowed impatiently to the sea but a maze of steel rails now crisscrossed the flats, carrying giant locomotives and assorted railcars to and fro. Railroad buildings crowded the stream banks and filled the valley.

On the bluff where the moose had wandered through the spruce were streets, numbered and lettered, lined with houses, filled with people. Beneath the dormer of a red-trimmed bungalow an infant slept. The railroad had brought change to Alaska, and to Mac.

List of Key Sources

Anderson, Anton A. *Construction and Maintenance Problems Encountered on the Alaska Railroad*

Anderson, Anton A. *Railroad Engineering Under Sub-Arctic Conditions*

Bernhardt, Joshua. *The Alaska Engineering Commission, Its History, Activities and Organization.* Institute for Government Research, Service Monographs of the United States Government, No. 4 New York, London: D. Appleton and Company, 1922

Brovald, Ken. *Alaska's Wilderness Rails, From the Taiga to the Tundra*, Pictorial Histories Publishing Co., Missoula, MT 1982

Cohen, Stan. *Rails Across the Tundra.* Pictorial Histories Publishing Co., Missoula, MT 1984

Crittenden, Katherine Carson. *Get Mears!* Portland, Oregon: Binford and Mort Publishing, 2002

Fitch, Edwin M. *The Alaska Railroad.* New York: Praeger, 1967

Prince, Bernadine LeMay. *The Alaska Railroad*, 2 volumes. Anchorage, AK: Ken Wray Printing, 1964

Service, Robert W. *The Spell of the Yukon and Other Verses*

Williams, Anita and Ewers, Linda D. *Rail Guide to the Historic Alaska Railroad*, Westours McKinley Explorer, Turnagain Products, Anchorage, AK

Wilson, William H. *Railroad in the Clouds: The Alaska Railroad in the Age of Steam, 1914-1945*. Boulder, CO: Pruett Publishing, 1977

Wohlforth, Charles *From the Shores of Ship Creek, Stories of Anchorage's First 100 Years*, 𝕿𝖔𝖉𝖉 𝕮𝖔𝖒𝖒𝖚𝖓𝖎𝖈𝖆𝖙𝖎𝖔𝖓𝖘, Anchorage, Alaska

---

Alaska Railroad Record, Official publication of the Alaska Engineering Commission, Vol. I and Vol. II

Alaska Railroad Corporation, Office of the Chief Engineer, Track Chart, Revised 1995

Friends of the Tanana Valley Railroad, *History of the Tanana Valley Railroad*

Hearings Before The Committee on Territories, House of Representatives, Sixty-Third Congress, First Session, On Bills H.R. 1739, H.R. 1806, and H.R. 1245, Wednesday, July 9, 1913

Hearings Before The Committee on Territories, House of Representatives, Sixty-Sixth Congress, First Session, On H.R. 7417, July 23, 24, 25 and 31, 1919

Railway Routes in Alaska, Report of the Alaska Railroad Commission, Washington, 1913

Reports of the Alaska Engineering Commission. The Period from March 12, 1914 to December 31, 1915

Society of the Chagres, *Builders of the Panama Canal, Yearbook 1916-1917*, Collected, Compiled and Edited by F. G. Swanson, Secretary Treasurer of the Society, Balboa, Canal Zone, Press of Girard Job Shop, Girard, Kansas